Eric Arvin

Wave Goodbye to Charlie

Eric Arvin

WILDE CITY
PRESS

WILDE CITY PRESS

www.wildecity.com

Wave Goodbye To Charlie © 2014 Eric Arvin
Published in the US and Australia by Wilde City Press 2014

Published by Wilde City Press

ISBN: 978-1-925180-48-0

Cover Design and Illustration by John Coulthart

www.johncoulthart.com

DEDICATION

Dedicated to the "Crack Crew".

Part 1

There's an abandoned carnival on the outskirts of town. Parts of it are still standing. The entrance is a large castle-like structure, the years having stripped away most of the siding on the towers by way of storms and winds so that now all that's left of them resembles arthritic bones reaching into the sky, all crooked and deformed. But on the lower levels of the castle, the remaining stone looks as cool as death in the moonlight. Most of the lettering has done fallen off the sign, but there is still a charred imprint over the gate that reads "Carnival."

This is my home.

I live here among these fading memories, a few miles east of Devlin, along a forgotten tree-lined county road that don't get much use at all but for curious teenagers or people up to no good. One of these days, we're gonna get a strong enough wind through here it's gonna blow this dirt road right off the map. It ain't but dust and gravel anyway. I ain't complaining, though. This is an ideal location, an ideal situation, for me. Living here, I ain't bothered by the noises and pollutions of living in town. When I need work or to get some food or pick up something to read, it's not too far a walk for me into Devlin. Sometimes, though, I will admit that walk can get downright creepy under all those trees. I've never liked trees. I don't trust what might be hiding in them or behind them.

Here in the carnival, I feel safe as houses. Home is where you hang your hat, and if I had a hat, well, this is where I'd hang it. I make the rules. I can sleep anywhere I want, whether it be in the old log ride—where I currently reside—the haunted house, or one of the freaks' tents. Just got to be careful, is all. Lots of places are falling down. The carnival ain't been open for years, and so it's just me and some of the old flags waving at each other in the wind. Mostly. Sometimes, though, the amusements turn on by themselves, and that gives me pause to think I may not be as alone as I think. The light bulbs above the Whac-A-Mole flitter on, the tea cup ride starts whirling round, the sign advertising the freak show burns bright, all sudden like and at once. At first, I was kinda freaked out by all that. It even made me think about leaving. But where would I go? I have no family. The carnival turns on later in the night anyway, and only for an hour, so I just lay there in my log and I listen to it until I fall back to sleep. There's a lullaby in creepy carnival music if you listen for it, and it don't tell of deformed babies chasing after you, wanting to gnaw on your leg.

* * * *

My name's Charlie, by the way. I'm many things, though none of them having to do with any real talent. I'm a runaway, a hustler when I need to be, a ghost when I have to scare hoodlums away from my home, and a loner who maybe reads too much. But most of all, I'm the keeper of the carnival. That's how I see myself. I look after the place 'cause even dying things need to be cared for. Maybe it's illegal. Maybe that rusty metal fence around the carnival is supposed to keep me out too. Or maybe me and this place were meant to find each other. Truth is, I never felt at home anywhere but here, not even in all the foster families and orphanages I was placed in as a young shit. They don't look for me no more, those places. I suspect I ran away so much they finally just said, "Fuck! Let him go." I am a hangnail on society's manicured middle finger. I'm older. One year past the age anyone gives a shit.

Well, most anyone. There is Trent. He seems to be warming up to me.

Trent is another hustler like me. New to the area, he lives in the city with another boy. We met one night at a café. We'd both just finished with tricks. The place was filled with truck drivers and drunks, none of whom seemed to care for our company. We found a booth in the back, though we hadn't said two words to each other. Recognition, you know. We were in the same circumstance. If you're gonna be judged, it's safer not to be judged alone. We hit it off and soon were laughing so loud we were thrown out of that fine establishment. I don't laugh much, but Trent, he's got a way about him. He's charming as a blue jay.

Lately, he's been coming to see me at the carnival. One night in Devlin, I let it slip I live there. I try to keep that hush-hush. I think it's sweet, though. I never had someone with a crush on me before, and the way he stares at me I can tell that's what it is. My, my, that boy's got big eyes and a cherub's face. How did he end up on the street? What no-good bastard would put him out? Tonight the two of us are walking the old county road beneath the tall twisted trees, and there's a big ol' moon that's hanging in a field of stars like it's fixed up there just for us. That's the romantic in me showing up. Sometimes I imagine things that can't ever be real. Sometimes it looks like those old tree branches are holding up Miss Moon all by themselves.

We pass slowly, meandering-like with our hands in our jean pockets, beneath the vines and the Spanish moss hanging from the limbs. It's like them trees was caught melting in the humidity. They will continue to melt once we pass on by. The katydids are drowning out the crickets tonight, but that's been the way of things this summer. Those with the loudest voices are always heard better even if they have nothing to say.

The county road is as twisted as these old trees, twisted and long and never seeming to truly go anywhere. Sure, the road leads into Devlin, if that's the way you're headed, but Devlin's not really anywhere at all but a wannabe town that's not got the gumption to be a gottabe town. It's just a dot on the map.

The summer heat is less oppressive in the night, but me and Trent are still sweating through our tank tops. He's holding my hand now, something that happened without me even realizing it, and we are congealed. I don't mind it, though. Hand-holding is something brand new to me, but I kinda like it. Even when it's hot and my palm is sweaty.

"You ain't got no neighbors for miles around, you say?" he asks me, his eyes as wide as if I was telling him a fairy story. "Go on now."

"I swear it, not for miles," I reassure him. "Besides the young fellas living in the old carnival caretaker's house just down that way, the only other folk who live anywhere near are an old black woman and a big bruiser with a mean truck. The old woman lives deep in the woods and never comes out. And I keep clear of the road usually, so I never see bruiser."

"Why do you keep clear of the road, Charlie?"

"Roads tend to lead places I don't want to go."

"But I'm not talking about any old road," says Trent. "I'm talking about this road, the road into Devlin."

"Or out of it."

"Sure, sure. Or out of it. Why keep clear of it? Now you answer me true."

I shrug with a smile. "I got no reason to be on it unless I'm heading to Devlin to do business or get food, and even then I can take shortcuts through the woods."

"But you're on it now."

"Well," I say, my voice ringing with charisma, "I got a reason now, don't I?"

This makes him blush. God bless you, Miss Moon, for letting me see it too. It's enough to make me want to ask him to come back to the carnival with me to stay a few nights. But I know he can't. He's got a roommate back in town, an ugly one, so it's Trent's hustling that pays the bills. And, too, not everyone can live in a carnival. Some people just get right freaked out by them. And Trent is new to hustling. He's easily freaked out.

"Do you believe in Heaven?" he asks me.

I look at him with a sly, oblique grin. "Is this a pickup line?"

"Just wondering," he says. "I do, and I think this feeling I got right now, it might be what Heaven feels like all the time."

"Ah, jeez, Trent." I blush for him. He probably thinks it's because he's so gosh darn romantic, and it kinda is. But it's also embarrassment for that cheese-ball line he just laid on me. Looking at that proud grin on his cherub face, though, I let him keep thinking what he wants.

He stops in the middle of the old gravel road and stares into my eyes. I'm a tall fella, so it's me who's looking down on him, but our eyes are lining up real nice. It's humid as all hell, and the bugs make it sound like we're in the belly of a frying pan. Swelter. That's what it is. Swelter and stickiness and we're all smiles for it. And when we kiss, it's like I took a bite of cotton candy, the kind I had at some other carnival years ago and far away. I only ever tasted cotton candy once, but this kiss is bringing it all back to me.

"Damn, Trent," I say. "That was nice. I ain't never kissed nobody and meant it."

He smiles at me, his dimples so deep a fella could fall into them. I hope that smile means he feels the same. It might be nice not to be so alone all the time.

I'm about to ask what he feels when I hear a rumbling and a grumbling speed up the road towards us. It's a truck, but dammit if it don't have some kind of vendetta. I keep tight to Trent's hand and try shielding my eyes with my free hand. Lights are blinding us as we stumble onto the shoulder of the road and wait for the beast to pass. But it doesn't pass. Instead, it stops at a curve so that its giant eyes are fixed on us and we can't see nothing else but their glare. Trent is clutching my arm now. I think he feels something ain't right.

"Stay calm," I tell him. "But prepare to run."

I hear the cab door open. The damn truck must be on tractor wheels like in them monster truck shows 'cause a pair of boots fall to the ground with a mighty clop. There's the sound of a chain rattling, pulling something, some living animal that don't sound too happy. The driver is standing in front of the lights now. I can't make him out, but the sound of the truck is familiar. This is one of my neighbors and a good reason I stay off the road. He stands silent for a minute, sucking on a big cigar by the looks of the smoke rising up around him. *Fuck*, I think. We're fucked. In one hand, he's got what looks like a shotgun, and in the other, he holds onto a chain that looks to be tied to an angry midget. But as I look closer, I see it's not a person at all, but a very muscular dog. The dog is growling and thrashing. He wants at us. He wants to rip us apart. The driver is simply jerking on the chain like it ain't no thing. I know Trent can feel me trembling.

"You boys are out late," says the driver. It's a sentence laid out flat. There is no hospitality in his voice. The very fact that we are out late has sealed us to some fate.

"We're just taking a walk, mister," I say, trying to talk above the truck. "It's a nice night for it. We'll head on home."

The driver looks around as if he is not certain it is, in fact, a nice night. "No," he says. "No, you won't be goin' nowhere. Boys like you don't have homes. Don't deserve homes."

The truck is roaring, the dog is tearing up the night, drowning out the bugs, the lights making me sweat all the more. Trent is tensing. He's ready to run, I can feel it.

"We ain't never done nothing to you, sir," I say. "Let us go. Please."

He laughs, and it sounds like something right out of hell. He spits his cigar to the ground, lets go the chain on the dog, and points the shotgun at me.

"No," he says.

"Run!" I shout as a shot is fired.

I swear I feel the bullet whiz right past my ear. Trent lets go of my hand. In a split second, I'm bounding down one of my shortcuts home, running as fast as my long legs can take me. The darkness is confusing, the trees suffocating. I'm thinking Trent is right behind me. It takes a minute to realize he ain't. He must be headed back towards town. I hear him screaming, crying, and getting farther away, but I can't go help. I can't even call out for him. The dog is after him, but that driver is after me. I hear him trampling through the brush with heavy boots in my wake. He fires every so often, but I'm doing good so far to evade getting an ass full of lead. I'm thin and wiry, and that driver has a lot more meat on his bones. All I need to do is tucker him out. Just keep running and tucker him out. I'm worried sick about Trent, though. That dog looked fucking hungry, and dammit if Trent wasn't the sweetest boy who ever lived.

Soon enough, I don't hear anything but the woods. I don't hear the driver running after me, I don't hear his truck, the dog, but most worrisome to me, I don't hear Trent. I slow down, almost out of breath. I am soaked through with sweat, and I'm breathing hard. I lean against a tree and look back, trying to see—hoping maybe Trent followed me somehow, that he outsmarted that big ugly dog and is gonna pop up from behind an oak and be all, "What do you think about all that?" But I know in my gut that ain't gonna happen. Even if Trent outfoxed that dog, the southern woods are tricky places. They can swallow a man whole in the daylight, let alone at night. Shadows are hungry things. Why do you think we've always got 'em dripping from our shoes?

I see a light and realize where I am. The little shack in the woods, the one that ain't much bigger than a toolshed, is just ahead. There resides another of my neighbors. The window is dark, but a lantern hangs from the plank that serves as a porch roof, giving the whole area a note of deadly welcome. But I ain't fooled. I don't want any more to do with neighbors. Not tonight. So I turn to leave…and run smack into the woman who belongs to that shack. Her name is Nessa, and she carries a spear. She's staring at me with wells of eyes like I done something wrong, like I coulda done something right. She keeps watch on me as I swivel around her and once again, with a few glances over my shoulder, race for my own home. For the carnival.

Through the woods, finally free of the trees and their ripping branches and tripping roots, I dip under the rusted chain link fence that's halfway to gone and keep running through the weeds, past the attractions, past the magician's parlor and the sideshow museum, past the Ferris wheel that's now little more than a planter, past the haunted house and the strongman's booth to the one place I feel safest of all, the one place no boogeyman, living or dead, will ever find me. The log ride. Here, out of breath and out of my mind with fright, I quickly climb the steps and hunker down in my favorite log, the one that's paused teetered over the waterfall drop with a view of all the fairyland people down below. I curl up in my old blankets and torn sheets and I shake and I cry and I pray. I pray for Trent. I'll go look for him tomorrow. Tonight I'm no use. Tomorrow I still won't be any good, but I can at least be useful during the day.

* * * *

I've awakened to the melody of the carnival. It must be two in the morning. Every night the carnival is alive for an hour—only an hour—and always at two. I don't know the why-fors. I've investigated, but I don't know much about mechanical stuff, and if there are ghosts here, real ghosts, I've never seen them. But at the stroke of two, the lights come on, the ones that work anyway, and the organ-style music of the games and the rides fills the air. At 2:59, it all goes off again, and the night is as silent as the pause after a threat.

I lay in my log and I listen. I'm still shaken by what happened to me and Trent. I want to go look for him, but that would be pointless in the dark. The trees have probably grabbed him up by now. If he's smart, he's hiding in the forest and didn't try and run back to Devlin. I don't know him well enough to recognize his intelligence, though.

I get up and make my way outside, to the lights and the carnival. The music is off-key and drooping, like it's rotting in the moonlight. Everything here needs a tune-up. The lights have lost most of their color too: shades of yellows and reds, but mostly dim white. I walk through the weeds and tree sprouts that now grow where people once crowded. The lights and the music combined with the shadows are playing tricks on my already frazzled nerves. If I didn't know better, I'da sworn I just saw something out of the corner of my eye. I'da sworn I saw lots of somethings. Dammit, if I think too long on it and let my mind wander the darkness, I'd be chased clear out of my carnival by made-up boogeymen. The only thing that's really ever creeped me out about carnivals and circuses—and I am not alone in this—is clowns. I can't stand 'em. So when I decided to squat here, the first thing I did was go around and find every last remnant of clown and toss it in a big ol' bonfire at the far end of the carnival grounds. I stay away from that ash pile now. That's unholy ground.

But sometimes I have bad dreams. Sometimes I see those burnt statues and signs rise up in the night and come for me while I sleep. They're smiling still.

I go through the maze, the rusty railings that force the line to "wait your turn" up to the merry-go-round. I sit on the platform and cross my legs, watching the menagerie of once-brilliantly colored animals pass by me. The drugged-out music fits the look of the poor creatures going round and round: horses without ears, tigers without claws, ostriches without heads, unicorns without reason. This is a carnival on the fringes. Every night for an hour it whispers, "I'm still here, world. Don't forget me." But it's too late. The world's moved on. Everyone wants quick thrills these days. No one's got time for rides on fake lions.

I sit here until three. I'll be witness to my carnival's plea for attention. At 2:59, it stops, as if someone unplugged the place. Everything freezes, the lights go out, and music shuts off. I'm left in the dark and my carnival is dead, a faint echo of its passing only slightly audible for the briefest of moments. Katydids drown out the rest. This makes me sad. The bear on the merry-go-round has stopped in front of me. He only has half a face, the rest broken off or chipped away. How's a bear supposed to roar with only half a face?

* * * *

I rise and look around for something to fill my time with until the sun comes up. I'm trying not to think on Trent. There's not much to do here I ain't already done. I visit the hall of mirrors in the fun house, always good for a laugh. Only I don't feel much like laughing and most of the mirrors are cracked and broken. I stand outside and stare at the haunted house for a bit—this big ol' gray thing that's starting to look scarier now than it ever did while in use—but decide against going in. Anything in there will only make me more anxious. Them lacquered-up mannequins that was left behind in there can get a might creepy even in the day.

I finally resort to just strolling around the carnival, listening to the wind shake the rusty metal go-carts and the loose wood on those structures that are still standing. Sometimes, when there's a strong enough breeze through the weeds, it's like the carnival has come to life. Picked right back up where it left off so long ago.

The sun is just peeking over the horizon, and one of those strong breezes is rolling through now, whipping my hair with some ferocity. I turn as the weeds rush all around me and the metal scrapings make a ruckus from the rides, and I think I hear a voice. Sounds like Trent. Just there, beyond the fence, beneath that massive oak tree, I swear I see a figure. I'm running towards it, jumping over weeds, debris, and twisted metal from storms long past. I'm at the fence, and the wind has died. There's no sign of a figure. No sign of Trent. I search the shadows, but nothing. I feel like a fool, letting my mind deceive me like that. It's light enough now, though. I'm gonna go look for him.

The trees in the woods are full of life. The birds put on a show…or throw a fit. Whichever you're in the mood for, that's what you hear. But the trees themselves, ornamented as they are with the moss and the song, are nonetheless dormant giants. During the day, they sleep, they replenish themselves. But at night, they play with shadows. I don't think I'd want to live in the woods. I mean, sure, me and my carnival are protected by trees. Nobody knows we're here. But I couldn't live among them. You never know what a tree is up to. That may sound crazy, but people believe in all sorts of crazy things: angels, aliens, devils, gods. How is what I believe any crazier than those? I'll stay in my headspace, you stay in yours.

Back on the road now, I can't see any proof me and Trent were even here last night. I don't know what I was thinking I would find coming back here. And honestly, if I did find something—say, an article of Trent's clothing— that would have just made me worry more. Now, I can at least tell myself Trent got away, hid out in the woods, and then hightailed it back to Devlin when the coast was clear.

Maybe Leroy and Jimmy saw something. Maybe Trent's even staying there with them. That's a thought and a damn comforting one too. Leroy and Jimmy are good folk. They'd take good care of him. Yes, sir. Wouldn't that be something if Trent was staying with them. If he's not with them and if I haven't heard from him by tomorrow, well, then I'll head to town. I'll find him, one way or another.

* * * *

Jimmy and Leroy live in an old house that's so big it feels like its approaching you as you're approaching it, like the damn thing's got legs. It looms. It's probably always loomed, even when it was newly built a thousand years ago for the carnival keeper. If at one time, though, it seemed awe-inspiring or threatening, now it only seems to need a paint job and a good weeding. Jimmy and Leroy don't seem too concerned with how the old place looks, how the lawn is no doubt home to snakes and other nasty critters. On either side of the dirt walkway leading up to the house are weeds and tall grass, interspersed here and there with wildflowers. It's a good thing they ain't looking to sell the place. There are some beautiful wildflowers, though. There's some orange and wild pink, even some bright blue, all mixed in with some of Queen Anne's lace. I once asked Jimmy if he wanted me to cut the grass for them, but he said there wasn't no sense in doing that. It'd just grow back, and why would I want to cut such pretty flowers anyway?

"It'd make the place look nicer," I said with a shrug.

"You mean it'd make the place look less chaotic," Jimmy'd answered. "Life is chaos, my young friend. And there's beauty in that."

I don't know about any of that. I suppose my life looks pretty chaotic, too, to outsiders looking in. While my life is comfortable to me, I don't particularly see any beauty in it. But honestly, by offering to cut the grass, I was just wanting to pay Jimmy and Leroy back for all the breakfasts and dinners they give me. I don't recall eating better in my life. Leroy can cook shit and make it taste like steak.

"Good mornin', there!" Jimmy hollers at me. He's on the front porch in the swing with an iced tea. I can hear the ice clink against the glass as he raises it to me. "You're out and about early." And without even asking me if I want to stay for breakfast, he shouts inside, "Leroy!"

There's no response. Jimmy takes a sip of his tea and swings lightly. I climb the steps to the porch and lean against the wood banister.

He shouts again, this time with a hint of exasperation. "Leroy!"

"What?" comes a deeper and even more exasperated voice from inside the house.

"Fix another place at the table, will ya?"

Leroy's voice changes, and it's all surprised and delighted…but still deep. "Is our boy Charlie here?"

Jimmy smiles at me. "He is indeed, and he looks like he's starvin' to death. Ain't you been eatin', Charlie boy?"

"Well, get on in here, Charlie," says Leroy. "And bring that old layabout in with you. He's been a good-for-nothin' all mornin'."

"Yessir," I say with a smile. These two make me laugh. I've never known any pair of human persons more comfortable with one another or more perfectly matched, from flowers to farts. Jimmy and Leroy accept one another wholly. That's the way it seems to me, anyway.

I don't see Trent, and my heart is sinking for it. Still, he probably just made his way back to Devlin. And I can get these fellas to help me search the woods just in case he's still hiding out in there. All I can do is pray he's not in that ugly dog's belly.

There's lots of space in this drafty house. If it weren't for the sunny dispositions of Jimmy and Leroy, the guts of the place would probably feel as downtrodden and in need of repair as the outside. As it is, there's not a lot of furniture.

There's a bureau here, a chair there. The living room has a big ugly green couch right in the center in front of the fireplace. There's an end table made out of piled newspapers next to it. But the rest of the room looks to be a gathering place for phantom furniture and paintings, the walls so old you can see the exact shape of the antique gun cabinet that used to be over there or the dullness of the framed portrait that once hung here. In the morning light, it don't look so bad. There's even a bit of charm to it. At night…well, night's another matter altogether. Like the woods, I have a feeling this old house has secrets that come alive at night, secrets I'd rather not hear whispered in my ears.

Leroy greets me with a smile in the kitchen in a sweaty white t-shirt, and suddenly he doesn't look as sick as I know he is. His good looks are hanging on by a thread, though. A fan oscillates behind him as he dries the perspiration from his brow, and the golden morning sunlight cheers up the room. How he has the strength to cook breakfast every morning is a mystery to me, but according to Jimmy, he insists on it. Says it keeps him going. Says if all he had pushing him to live was Jimmy, he'da been dead yesternoon. He says this with a sly grin and a wink to Jimmy. Jimmy harrumphs whenever Leroy says this. There's a lot of harrumphing between these two, god love 'em.

The kitchen is the only room in the house that looks lived-in. It's a right mess from Leroy's cooking, and boy, can he cook! The table is set like they're expecting seven dwarves. There's pancakes piled high as buildings, toast as thick as bricks, fluffy eggs you could sleep on, crisp bacon, spicy sausage, and a few things I ain't never heard of but taste so damn good I'm afraid to ask what they're called. If Heaven has a smell, it's just like Leroy's kitchen.

"Sit down, Charlie boy," says Leroy. "Sit down and have at it, or else I'm gonna have to hand you a mop and bucket to clean up your drool."

Truer words ain't never been spoken. I'm salivating.

I'm having me a little bit of everything, dipping my sausage in the syrup, wrapping my eggs up in my pancakes, and washing it down with a big glass of milk. You'd think I'm dying of starvation by how fast I'm eating. It's so much better than the crap I usually eat, though, I can't help myself.

"Look at our boy go, Leroy," says Jimmy, taking a break from eating so he can watch me. "Shooey, I never seen no one eat like that."

Truth is, neither of them is really old enough for me to be their "boy," but I don't mind it. For the past year, since they moved into the old place, this has been my own personal bar & grill. They always give me leftovers, too, and they never ask for anything in return. We have a connection, I think. I feel like they're runaways, too, of some sort. They don't have a family either.

"With that appetite," says Jimmy, "where do you find the food to keep yourself alive? You're skinnier than a twig and most likely burn through calories faster than you can eat 'em. You only eat here two or three times a week." He leans towards me. "You cheatin' on us?"

I shrug. "I make do," I say while destroying a piece of coffee cake dripping in brown sugar sauce. "I got canned foods back at the carnival. Walls of cans. They're pretty cheap at the Dollar Tree. I also got some cereals and chips. And sometimes a trick will even give me some extra cash for a meal. Sometimes they'll take me out to dinner, too, if they really liked what I did."

I can feel Leroy and Jimmy look at each other over the table without having to see them. Their glances have drafts of unease.

"Are you sure you wouldn't rather come here and live with us?" asks Jimmy. "We got plenty of room, Charlie boy. You wouldn't even have to hustle no more."

"And you'd get good food every day," says Leroy. "You'd wake up to the smell of fried eggs every morning and go to sleep with a full stomach every night. Lasagna, pizza, fried chicken, whatever you want."

I take a big swallow of everything in my mouth. It hurts good going down. "That's real nice of you fellas," I say (and I've said it before), "but I like the carnival. I like my space there. I guess I'm just an independent soul, is all." I look at both of them, hoping they understand. We have this conversation, or something similar to it, every other week.

Jimmy smiles and hits me on the shoulder. "Just be careful there," he says. "Leroy's a big mother hen. He'd hate to see you come to any harm." Leroy isn't saying anything, but he's still smiling.

To be honest, I might have considered living with them. They're great guys and having a group of friends, a tribe, would be a new experience. Maybe I'd even like it. If only their home wasn't *this* home. The old carnival caretaker's place is fine for morning breakfasts and quick visits, but it's dark here, haunted by things much darker than the carnival itself. I feel things watching me every time I'm here, even now as I'm polishing off this meal. I wonder why Leroy and Jimmy don't feel it. But then again, maybe they do and that's why they want me to move in, to help them beat back the haunters. I'd say something about what I feel, but I'm afraid they'd take it the wrong way, like I was just being ungrateful or something, making excuses.

I finish off my milk while I'm finishing off my thoughts. I came here for a reason, and it's nearly been forgotten.

"Either of you fellas seen another guy around here about my age?" I ask. "We ran into trouble last night on the county road, and we got split up. I ain't seen him since, and I'm real worried."

"Naw, just you," answers Jimmy. "Does this trouble you speak of drive a noisy truck and have an ill-tempered dog?"

"That's the one," I say. "I've done well avoiding him until now."

"I don't know what his proper name is, but we call him Bull," says Jimmy, "on account of the way he looks. He's a right mess. You ain't plannin' on going snoopin' round that big bruiser's place to search for your friend, are ya? That I would not recommend."

"Naw. I'm betting Trent just found his way back to Devlin. That's what I hope, anyway. I'm heading there tonight. I've got a weekly trick in town, and we're usually done early enough for me to take my time getting home before it gets too dark. I'll go check on Trent at his apartment, if I can remember how to get there."

"Is that what you're wearin'?" asks Leroy. He's not being facetious or nothing. Just concerned.

I look down at myself. My tank top is soiled a nice brown and stiff with last night's sweat. My jeans are just as filthy and torn in at least five places. I'm surprised Leroy let me into the house.

"You need some new clothes is what Mama Leroy is sayin'," says Jimmy.

"And a bath," says Leroy. "You're spicier than these sausages, Charlie boy."

Jimmy stretches and rises to his feet. He is not as tall as me, but broad-shouldered and a country girl's idea of handsome. "Come on upstairs. We'll get you cleaned up. I'll find somethin' from my closet for you to wear tonight while you get in the tub."

"Then maybe you should take a nap," says Leroy. "You'll get run over walkin' into town with as little sleep as you've had."

"Don't argue with him." Jimmy can no doubt see the objection rising in my face. "Won't do no good. Leroy won't let you out of the house without layin' a guilt trip on ya if you try and escape. Then I'll get it, too, for lettin' ya go."

* * * *

I just woke up from a midday dream. A nightmare really.

I took Leroy's advice and had a nap, though not in the house. I made up some excuse about not being able to sleep in a proper bed after living so long in the carnival—which of course ain't true. I can sleep anywhere and through anything. But in the end, I convinced Leroy I'd be fine sleeping on the steps of the porch outside, my back against the banister. Truth is, I needed it. I was worn out.

I feel real clean now too. I haven't taken a bath, not a real bath in a real tub with clean water, in a long time. There's a small creek beside the carnival, just off in the woods, and I wash myself clean there when I get too rank. When the creek's not running, I use the collected rainwater from the tin buckets I position around the carnival just for that purpose. But this is a whole new clean for me. I feel crisp and sparkling. Leroy washed my clothes while I was bathing, and Jimmy set me out something new to wear tonight like he said he would. My new clothes—new to me, anyway—

are folded up neatly beside me here on the steps and they smell all grown-up and fragrant, like Jimmy's cologne. I feel like a damn prince.

The midday heat is causing me to sweat again, though, taking away some of that crisp, sparkly feeling, and the katydids and summer bugs are trilling something awful. Sometimes a fella's got to shout to be heard over them. Jimmy and Leroy are both up in the porch swing. They're napping and swaying back and forth so that the swing's chain makes a tiny chirp of its own, like it's in chorus with the bugs. I'm sitting here, eyes open, trying to piece together the dream I just had. Something about fire, about fear. I was scared to death in that dream, but now it's fading fast from my mind like it wasn't nothing. That's fine by me. There's too much to be scared of in the waking world to have to worry about dreams.

I get up and stretch out my kinks, trying not to disturb Jimmy and Leroy. I pack the clothes in under my arm and start heading down the overgrown walkway. I need to go get ready for tonight.

"What do you think you're doing?" Jimmy is awake and standing at the banister. "Ain't you gonna say goodbye to us? Don't we even get a wave?"

"I didn't want to wake you," I say. "You looked so peaceful. Like big burly babies."

"Hush your mouth," Jimmy says with that shit-eatin' grin. He turns to Leroy, who is still very much asleep and snoring. "Leroy," he calls out. "Leroy!"

"Wh-what the hell do you want, Jimmy?" asks Leroy, being dragged unceremoniously from his slumber. "I was dreamin' of naked muscle men, all bent over and offering me their backsides."

"You dirty fucker," Jimmy says, shaking his head. "Wave goodbye to Charlie. He's headed back to the carnival."

"Headed home, Charlie?" asks Leroy.

"Now ain't that what I just said?" Jimmy jibes. "I swear to god…"

"Yessir," I say. "Need to get dressed and ready before I head into town. Thanks for breakfast. And the new clothes. I'm gonna look kinda splendid tonight."

Leroy is standing beside Jimmy now. "You come back any time you want, hear me? It's nice to cook for someone besides this big slob. He don't seem to appreciate a thing I do."

"Huh…" says Jimmy.

"I hope you find your friend, Charlie boy," says Leroy. "We'll keep our eyes open for him just in case he comes stumblin' out of them woods."

"And you be careful." Jimmy's face now is what I think a father's should look like: hard but concerned. "Don't let yourself run into that Bull."

I give them a final wave, and I head off through the woods along one of the many shortcuts I know to the carnival. The forest is filled with noisy critters, bugs and birds. Butterflies flitter before me, but moths flap in my face. Gnats and flies drawn to the scent of my sweat and Jimmy's cologne clamber around me in annoying circles. I climb over fallen trees that look like bent arms and elbows and small deformed stumps that resemble little elves or dwarves. I'm on the lookout, though. No whistling or carefree trotting. If there's a sign of Trent, I don't want to miss it. Same goes for Bull.

The carnival fence is just ahead. There's somebody standing there, like they're waiting for me. *Could be Trent*, I think to myself, all excited. If it is, he's gonna get the hugging of his life. Other than Jimmy and Leroy, Trent is the only one who knows where I live. I start to walk faster, almost shouting his name, when I think, *What if it's Bull?* That stops me dead in my tracks.

But the figure is too thin to be Bull, and there ain't no mean dog nearby either.

"Who are ya?" I ask from where I stopped in the woods. "What do you want? I ain't got nothing."

The figure looks at me and starts walking. As it approaches, I can see it's not Trent or Bull. It's the old black woman who lives in the woods. The witch. Only she ain't really all that old, maybe she's in her fifties, but she's got a real youngish look to her. She's got long hair speckled with gray, and she's wearing a tank top and faded blue jeans. She looks harmless. Well, except for her eyes. Her eyes are intense. She might be able to tear a man apart with those eyes, with the hurt, the hate, the anger I see in them. It's them that make me back up a few steps.

"The name's Nessa," she says to me, standing nearly as close as when I ran into her last night. "Are you Charlie?"

I swallow. "Yes, ma'am," I say. The lack of feeling in her voice throws me. "I-I'm Charlie."

"I've been hearing messages," she says. "Things that are meant for you. From your friend Trent. He ain't gonna leave me alone until I relay 'em, I suppose. He wants you to know he's fine. He's just fine now. You don't need to look for him. Everything is fine."

"Trent?" I say, relieved. "You've seen Trent? Ah, that's great news, Miss. Can you take me to him? I'd sure like to see him."

The stoic look on her face changes to one of confusion. "You can't see him no more," she says. "Now best you forget about him. Best you carry on with your days." She slowly slides past me and begins to walk deeper into the woods.

"And Charlie," she says, turning back around, "stay off the road. You're safer in the trees, no matter what you think."

I didn't need to ask her "safer from whom."

But I'm left wondering why Trent don't want me looking for him. Has he found someone else to crush on? Did some fella come along last night and save him from Bull's dog? It don't make no sense.

When I showed Trent the carnival, brought him here for the very first time, he wasn't impressed by the old rides or games. He didn't want to go into the fun house or the castle gate. He just wanted to walk around with me.

"Don't you wanna see anything?" I asked him. "There's some real freaky stuff in the haunted house."

He shrugged. "I don't need to see that," he said with his dimpled grin. "Unless you need me to see it."

"I don't need you to see anything."

"Good. Because I like this. I like just walkin' around with you, Charlie. Does that make me strange?"

"Naw," I said. "I think it's real sweet. Why, you're like a piece of candy, you are, Mr. Trent."

We might have even kissed right then if, at that very moment, part of the old food booth we were standing in front of hadn't collapsed, pushed over by the wind. I pulled Trent out of the way just before a slab of tin would have most certainly cut his Achilles heel.

"Well, what in the world," he said in hushed excitement as he surveyed the scene. Then he looked right into me and said, "I got myself a certified hero."

"Shucks," I said. "I ain't nothing like that. I just got an eye for disaster, I guess."

"Naw, Charlie," he said. "You're a hero. You're a regular Superman."

That made me feel real good at the time. Now I'm left wondering, though, if I'm such a hero, why don't he want me around no more?

* * * *

Patricia sits up on her big feather pillows that are covered in satin, and leans against a massive headboard. She is indifferent to the world, and her black dress (always black) is so free of wrinkles you'd think we hadn't just done what she pays me to come here and do. The bedcover is pulled away, and her dress is now fanned out over her useless legs like she's a china doll on a shelf.

She's not been able to walk for years, though I don't know the tale. That would require a closeness me and Patricia don't have, nor should we. She's a client, that's all. All I know is there was a man and he is somehow to blame.

She requires my services once a week, the same day every week, the same hour of that day, and in that hour we do the same thing, no variations, and then I leave. It seems like it's a chore or something she has to do, not something she truly desires. I don't think Patricia smiles. I've never seen anything of this large old townhouse—she calls it "Italianate," as if that's supposed to impress me—other than the front parlor and her bedroom here on the ground floor. I imagine it all looks pretty much the same: dimly lit and colorless, dripping with anger. She has a nurse, but I don't see much of him. He's a good-looking fella, though, tall, broad-shouldered, and thick-armed. He's very pretty, a lot prettier than me. Patricia likes to surround herself with pretty things. But like everything else here, he seems sad, like he's in mourning and couldn't crack a smile if he wanted to. Maybe that's why she likes him so much. Or rather, tolerates his company. I don't know if Patricia actually likes anyone.

She watches me dress. A lot of my clients and tricks do. I'm cleaner than she usually sees me. Don't get me wrong. I take a bath and wash what needs washing, but I don't usually smell like flowers. She remarked on this when her nurse escorted me into the room to see her. I don't know if she approves of my new look.

"Are you in love?" she asks me now as I pull on my shirt. Her blonde hair is perfect as it sits on her thin shoulders. "Is that why you smell like a perfume factory? Has someone captured that hustling heart of yours?" She is brittle, but her voice is still loaded with cynicism.

"No, ma'am," I say, startled by this bit of personal interest on her part.

"Strange. You look to me like someone in love. You've cleaned yourself up. You've never done that for me before. There's a restless glow about you as well. Are you certain you are not in love?"

"Who would I be in love with, ma'am?" I answer. Trent's face flashes through my mind ever so quickly. "I live by myself. In my line of work, falling in love would be—" I see Trent's smile, his dimples in my mind. "—silly, pointless."

"I would have to let you go, you know. If you ever fell in love, that is. Even if it was me who was the object of your affection. I would have to let you go. I would need to find someone else to provide me these services."

This, as if I am on her staff.

"I ain't in love." I state it clearly this time.

"Love is a terrible thing, Charlie. People tell you it's wonderful. They'll tell you of thunderstorms and lightning and love at first sight, but they're all fools. Fools or liars. Love only leads to tragedy, heartache, and anger. So much damn anger. Love never works. You think it will when you're deep in it, when you think you've found the perfect man. But it's a ruse. Like everything in the world"—she touches her legs—"love has its breaking point."

"But sometimes it works." I'm standing in front of her, ready to go, but feeling the need to defend love.

She looks at me curiously, as if she had just caught me in a lie. "No, Charlie. Love will only leave you alone in the end. And then you'll do the most awful things to try and shut it up, to quell the pain that it has caused when it tore you to pieces. You'll hurt others, and in time, you won't even feel bad about that. Do you understand?"

What was I to say? "Yes, ma'am."

"I don't believe you." She sighs. "But you'll learn the truth, I suppose. You'll learn just who you can use, who you can take advantage of to survive this demon called love. Don't say I didn't warn you, Charlie. Your money is by the door."

I pick up my payment on the way out. I am perfectly aware I am one of those Patricia is using.

"Do you like music, Charlie?" she asks as I step into the hallway.

"Yes, ma'am. I mean, I suppose."

"Music lovers are the only true souls in the world. If you don't listen to music, you don't have a soul. Beware of people who don't appreciate music, Charlie." Then she squints her eyes, as if thinking. "I think next week we'll have some music. What do you think? Won't that be nice? A concert just for you and me, here in this room."

I'm standing there, waiting for her to say more. Instead, she looks at me and says bluntly, "You may go."

I take my leave, walking faster than Patricia's nurse can usher me to the door.

Having been excused, I'm headed for Trent's apartment while there is still light out. Miss Nessa told me she had seen him in the woods and for some reason he didn't want me looking for him, but I have to make certain he is okay. I liked the guy. I'm sure he liked me too. Was that what Patricia had seen? Had my friendship with Trent made it seem I was in love? If so, she is way off the mark. I… appreciate Trent. That's all. I liked the attention.

I climb the rickety rail steps of the back-alley closet Trent shares with a revolving door of roommates. It's actually smaller than a closet, to be honest, a shoebox of a place that Trent has been turned out of for not paying rent at least three times in the last four months I've known him. Hustling ain't an easy living, especially in a town like Devlin. I knock on the beat-up white door that could easily be kicked in and shattered, but there's no answer. I try the knob, but there's no give. So I sit on the railing and wait for a good fifteen minutes for Trent or his roommate to show. All the visitors I get, though, are a calico cat with a breathing problem and a drunk looking for a good time. I give him a blow job and get three bucks for it.

Dusk is coming. I need to get back to the carnival so I don't have to walk through the woods in the dark. If I had a pen, I'd write Trent a note on his door. The paint job wouldn't mind. But I ain't got one, so after a few more minutes, I head on back home. Every so often I look over my shoulder, hoping I'll see Trent coming up behind, waving and telling me Miss Nessa misheard him. That I'm still his hero. Then I think, maybe he's still in the woods. Maybe he's unconscious and dying somewhere. Makes me sick to my stomach to think that while I was stuffing my face at Jimmy and Leroy's, Trent could have been somewhere dying. More

likely, though—and this hits me harder than I expected—
he's moved on to another town. That's why he didn't want
me looking for him no more. That's what my mind finally
settles on, and it's bringing me down. It's a good thing I'm
not in love with him, or else I'd be proving that crazy bitch
Patricia right. Love's a fucking demon.

I reach the woods just as the last glimmer of sun is in
the sky. My hands are in my jean pockets, and my face is
cast down. I'm not really thinking too hard on anything
when I suddenly get this wild hair—I don't know where it
came from—to see the other side, to see where Bull lives.
I think to myself, I oughta give him a piece of my mind
for scaring me and Trent like he did. With each step, I'm
angrier and more certain that a confrontation is exactly
what is needed. Bull will be shaking in his big boots when
he sees me coming. I swipe a thick branch from the ground
and clench it tight. Bull needs a good beating. Fuck his gun
and his dog.

* * * *

He lives in a stinking swamp. I'm in the shadows,
I'm part of the shadows, behind a warped tree. I'm now
feeling a bit uneasy. I'm shaking, breathing hard. The heat
is oppressive, and I'm a damn buffet for every mosquito
miles around. I look up. Everything is dark. I can't see the
sky through the thick tree branches and foliage. Like the
humid air, they're pressing down on me. That mean ol' dog
is carrying on something awful from his pen. He knows I'm
here. He can hear me past the night bugs. I'm probably the
only thing around here that doesn't smell like muck and
shit. Heck, I'm surprised Bull don't smell me yet. He's in
that sloppy-looking shack made from tin siding and wood.

Looks like Miss Nessa's place, but not as orderly. His big truck sits in front of it like an overfed gator. Tree stumps are scattered about, like the trees have been cut off so they can't escape the stinking air. Beneath that shit-laden air, there's a faint scent of ash and fire.

That dog won't shut up. I tighten my grip on the branch I found, and I swallow. My heart's about to explode. Suddenly, I'm a silly little boy. What was I thinking?

Shut up, Dog!

But he won't hush. He's rattling the fence and snarling and looking right at me, growing more crazed with every passing second. Bull slams open the door and comes out. I nearly shit myself.

"Fuckin' mutt!" he yells. He picks up a block of wood and throws it at the pen to get the dog to shut up, but the dog goes on barking. I can't move. My feet have grown roots. I'm a tree.

I have to confront this bastard about Trent. I gotta. That's what I'm here for. What's the worst he can do to me, anyway?

But it's like the dog has told him where to look. Like, exactly where to look. Bull narrows in on me. I don't even think he's squinting. I'm petrified wood. He lets loose this roar like a monster whose cave I've just wandered into. I piss myself, drop my branch, and run. I don't bother to look over my shoulder. I know he's after me. I know he's got that dog and is chasing me down through the woods 'cause I can hear him yelling and I can hear that mean ol' dog barking and snarling.

Shit! Fuck! Shit! Fuck! Shit! Fuck! It's a mantra in my head, and it correlates to every footfall.

I'm running fast as I can. Birds and bugs and things that only come out at night scream at my passing. I pray the trees and the shadows are on my side tonight. *Just hide me,* I'm asking them. *Please.*

But that dog is tracking me and Bull is calling out, "Come on out, boy! Ain't no use in hiding. Your skin is mine. I need a new rug."

I run, but where am I running? I can't go back to the carnival. I don't want Bull to know where I live. He'd track me down in no time if I ran there. So I'm heading for the only other place I feel safe. I cross a stream, hoping that will throw the dog off my scent, at least for a bit, maybe confuse him, and I head, full steam, for Jimmy and Leroy's. My eyes got the tunnel vision. I can only see what's in front of me, and it's getting blurry. I'm running hard.

I race up a wooded hill, onto the county road, and it takes a lot out of me, but there ain't no slowing down. *If there are any wood spirits, I could sure use your help. I don't want to be that dog's play toy or, worse, midnight snack. And I don't want to be Bull's fleshen rug in his shit shack.*

I'm back into the woods on the opposite side now, and I hear Bull closing in. Cutting through the trees on a brand new shortcut I'm making up as I go, my face is being swatted by limbs and branches, and damn, I can hardly breathe. It's Bull's voice that keeps pushing me, though. That dog is scary, but for some reason, I fear the Bull more.

Out of the woods and onto the gravel road that leads to Jimmy and Leroy's place, I start screaming, hollering for help, racing and fumbling. My legs are about to give out. I can't feel them anymore. But I'm shouting between each deep breath. The house looms up ahead. My hearing is clouded, my throat is closing in, but I think I'm safe. I think I've made it.

I'm on the dirt walkway, and suddenly, I'm tackled, feeling a set of vicious teeth sink into my right thigh. Crying out, I fall into the overgrowth and do my best to ward off the dog. My hands are a poor defense. I can hear Bull nearby. He's breathing hard, harder than me, but it sounds like he's laughing. He's gonna let the damn dog tear me apart. I can't differentiate now between the dog's growl and Bull's laugh. I'm gonna die. I'm gonna die right here.

A shot. A gunshot hits the ground near my head. I'm not hurt, but I scream. I'm thinking Bull is shooting at me, but another shot grazes the dog's ear and the hound jumps off me with a howl. I'm in such a state that I see the hair of the dog fall away in slow motion. I'm in a movie, I think. This is all fiction. Bull is yelling something, the dog is whimpering, and my thigh hurts like a motherfucker.

I see Bull ain't looking at me no more, and he ain't got a gun neither. But Jimmy does. He's on the porch with a shotgun, and it's trained right at Bull.

"Get the hell off my land," says Jimmy as he's coming towards us down the walkway. I never heard Jimmy so angry before.

"I don't want no trouble," says Bull, his hands raised. "I just want the boy. He's a trespasser. Needs to be punished, is all. Needs to be taught his place."

"By that thinkin', mister, so are you. You're on my land." The shotgun clicks. "Now, get off it."

"You gonna protect this piece of shit?"

"I'm a good shot, mister. Those two I fired were warnin' shots. I like dogs. Don't want to see no dog killed. I have no problem killin' asses, though. I'll give you to the count of three to turn around and hightail it off my land. I'll give you to four if you take that dog with you and tend to his wound."

The dog is hiding behind Bull, half snarling, half whining.

"You ain't gonna shoot me. I'm a man, just like you." Every word is spit out.

"Don't test me," says Jimmy.

"He may not shoot ya," comes a grizzled shout from a second floor window of the house, Jimmy and Leroy's bedroom where I had taken my bath earlier. "But I will." Leroy has a rifle aimed at Bull as well. "Shootin' a man ain't such a crime if that man deserves it." Leroy's voice is like a bear, so much like a roar that hairs are standing up on the back of my neck. I imagine a bear would defeat a bull easily in a fight.

"Alright, fellas," says Bull, backing off. "Alright. Two against one ain't fair, especially when that one is an unarmed man just lookin' to protect what's his. Ain't there no justice in the world?"

"Git!" hollers Leroy, his voice filling the air.

"Didn't realize there were more of his kind here. Y'all are all over the place, huh?"

"I said git." And with that, Leroy fires and hits the tip of Bull's right boot, causing the big man to jump and squeal. He and the dog are running so fast from our sight it'd be funny if I weren't so damn uncomfortable with pain. I wanted to yell to Leroy to keep shooting at the bastard.

"What the hell did you get yourself into?" asks Jimmy as he inspects my wound. "Didn't we tell you not to play with the livestock?"

"I was trying to be a hero," I say through gritted teeth, "trying to find my friend."

He offers me his shoulder, and we're hobbling to the porch.

"You okay there, Charlie?" shouts Leroy from above. He's still poised with his rifle at the window in case Bull decides to come back.

"He'll be fine," answers Jimmy. "Just got a case of the stupids."

"It didn't seem stupid when I first thought of it. I was just gonna go talk some sense into him, is all."

"Guys that ugly don't know how to talk sense. They traded any sense they had for more ugly."

"Man, am I glad you were here," I say, my nerves still jumping and chattering beneath my skin. "I would have been dog meat if not for you two."

"Well, I'm just glad our friend Bull didn't try and push his luck," says Jimmy as he helps me up the porch steps. "Truth is, I'm a terrible shot. I was aimin' for the dog's head. Leroy is a great shot, but he's sick in bed tonight. I thought he was asleep. He was probably shaky as a leaf holdin' his rifle."

"So," I say, "you could have shot me?"

Jimmy looks at me, shocked as all get-out. "Could never did, Charlie," he says. "It all worked out in the end, didn't it? You're alive, ain't ya? Huh. There's gratitude for ya. Get your ass inside before I send for Bull."

* * * *

The small kitchen fan is offering little relief from the humid nighttime air. That combined with all the running I just did makes me feel like I'm gonna explode in a big ball of fire. I've got a baggie full of ice on my neck to cool me down. Crickets and katydids are singing in through the screen door, and the smells of summer dusk are mingling with the scents of Leroy's kitchen: dewy grass, cinnamon biscuits, and hay. Leroy has me naked, up on the table, and is looking at my thigh. Jimmy makes a crack about buttered biscuits for tomorrow morning. This is the first time I can remember a fella's ever had me naked without an ulterior motive or a pocket full of cash. My dick is lying limp on the table between my legs, though, and I ain't got much to offer in way of payment. Leroy's got a basin, the water inside it the color of my blood, and he's cleaning my wound with rubbing alcohol. It stings so I hiss and jump.

"Serves ya right," he says, his voice deep with just a hint of annoyance. "What kind of fool goes to a bigoted drunk's house in the woods at night without any protection?"

"I had a stick."

He looks at me like he's gonna slap me upside the head. Jimmy does it for him from behind.

"What was that for?" I say.

"I apologize," says Jimmy. "I thought I saw some delusions in your hair."

The overhead light is so bright it's washing us all out. We don't look like we've spent a day in the sun between us. But most of all Leroy. I don't think I've seen him sicker. It's like he's gonna throw up or pass out just looking at the dog bite. He keeps cleaning it anyway, though, god bless him.

"I'm real sorry, Leroy," I say.

"For what?" he asks, his attention still on my thigh.

"For getting you out of bed. I know you're real sick." The alcohol stings, but I ain't letting my discomfort show.

Leroy looks up at me and he smiles. "Ain't you somethin'?" he says. Then up to Jimmy, "Ain't he somethin'?"

"He is that," Jimmy responds. I can hear the smirk in his voice. "He's a whole lot of somethin'."

"Charlie boy," says Leroy in his deep-as-coal voice, "do you know how many scrapes and tears I've had to mend for that sorry sonbitch right there behind you? He gets himself into more shit than a five-year-old at a shit-gettin' party. We can't go to bars because of his big mouth. And I've been in much worse states than this when I've had to patch him up, I assure you. Why, this lazy fucker damn near killed me once. Got himself high as a kite a few months back, then decided he was gonna rid the house of all the grays he saw, so he found his shotgun…"

"Grays?" I ask, looking up at Jimmy. Jimmy shrugs.

"He don't remember a damn thing about it now," says Leroy. "He just remembers wakin' up in bed with a bandaged foot from where he nearly shot off his big toe. He was bellyachin' for a week, I tell you what. He also don't remember thinkin' I was one of those grays. Said I had the pallor of a damned gray. Sonbitch."

"Don't do drugs, kids," adds Jimmy. "Sage advice."

"Sonbitch," Leroy mumbles, throwing the bloody wash rag into the basin. "Jimmy, why don't you quit your lurkin' about and go find me some bandages for our wounded hero here."

"Shit, Leroy. I dunno where you put the bandages. You're always movin' shit around this house. Ain't nothin' ever in the same place."

"The bandages are where they have always been, my forgetful friend. Upstairs bathroom, under the sink. In the white container. It reads 'Bandages'."

"Huh." Jimmy grunts as he leaves the kitchen. "I expect a beer when I get back." Leroy shakes his head and watches Jimmy go.

"Nearly shot me dead," he repeats to me in a lowered voice.

"Why are you two still together?" I ask. "I mean, you seem so frustrated with him all the time. You ain't planning on breaking up, are you? Please tell me you ain't."

"Ain't you somethin'?" says Leroy with a raised brow. "Don't you worry, Charlie boy. Mom and Dad ain't gettin' a divorce. This is just how we are, how we always have been with each other. We're a perfect match. Nobody else would be able to stand either of us. Love, dear Charlie, is a game of give and take. I wouldn't give him so much shit if I didn't think he could take it."

"How'd you two meet, anyhow?"

He sits back in a chair now, waiting for Jimmy to come back with the bandages. "We was both hired on at one of those high falootin' dormitory schools for boys. The kind that are so restrictive they trade freedom for rules and rules become oxygen. The kind of place that you would never have survived. I was the cook. Jimmy was the history teacher." I give him a surprised look, I guess, because he smiles and says, "Yeah. Crazy, huh? We're educated. Both of us come from pretty wealthy families too. Jimmy's family disowned him, though. He hasn't spoken to 'em in years. That happened long before he met me. We started at the school around the same time and clicked immediately. I grabbed onto his vibe and he grabbed on to mine, know what I mean? We kept it quiet for as long as we could, but things have a way of gettin' found out in a small school. Three years in and we were fired. Jimmy had told someone he was in love, and that someone put one and two together. Soon there was a panic in the hallowed halls of academia."

"That's not fair," I say. I have nearly forgotten about the pain in my thigh.

He coughs, hacking up something dark and vile. "No," he says, collecting himself. "It's not fair. But neither is it fair that a fine boy like you lives alone and without family in an abandoned carnival."

"Were you mad at Jimmy?"

"For what? For telling someone I was the only thing in the world that meant anything to him? Hell no. That's what you call romance, Charlie. No. The only thing I resent when I'm with Jimmy is that I can't be more a part of him than I am. You see, we're like one person in two bodies. When I'm mean or ornery to him, I'm just being self-deprecating, because we're the same. Understand?"

"I think so."

"You see, Charlie, love destroys the person you were, but that's not necessarily a bad thing."

Jimmy comes back into the kitchen. "Got the bandages," he says. "Where's my beer?"

Leroy takes them, stares at them, and says, "Well, dagnabbit, Jimmy. Where's the Neosporin? I can't very well wrap this up without Neosporin. It'll get infected. Where's your thinkin' head?"

"Man alive, Leroy! You didn't ask for it!"

"It was a layin' right there with the bandages. Right there. Now go back on up there and get it."

"Huh," groans Jimmy as he leaves us once again.

"I swear," says Leroy, shaking his head as he looks at me. "He's dumb as shit, but I do love him."

"I heard that!" yells Jimmy from the stairs.

* * * *

It's a beautiful day. The humidity has lessened its hold on the county and allowed me to do the work I promised I'd do for Jimmy and Leroy a few days ago. After Jimmy saved my skinny ass from Bull, I told the fellas I was gonna clean up their front yard for them whether they wanted me to or not. Cut the weeds, scare out the critters. I made sure to go through and collect any pretty flowers first, though, and I put them in a vase I found lying empty around the house. Leroy appreciated that and he put that vase as a centerpiece on the kitchen table. Made me feel special. Jimmy said I didn't have to do nothing for them. He said anybody would have done the same. But it was me who'd brought a bull to their quiet house. I hate the thought that I disturbed their peace, you know?

They have one of those old-timey push mowers, just blades and wheels, so it's a chore getting the lawn trimmed. I done took my tank top off and, I'll be honest, I'm tempted to do the same with the jeans. Ain't nothing more uncomfortable than heavy jeans when you're sweating. It's not like there's any neighbors to be shocked by my naked white ass. Every so often a nice breeze will blow through the surrounding trees, though. That offers some relief. There's supposed to be some rain later, so the local paper says.

"How's that thigh?" Jimmy asks, bringing me another glass of iced lemonade. He's a bit subdued today, like his mind is on a thousand other things.

"Oh, it's fine," I say, emptying the glass in a matter of seconds. I'll have to empty my bladder in the woods again before long. "It don't hurt none anymore. I've been keeping it clean, washing it every night, just like Leroy told me to."

"He'll be glad to hear it. So tell me this, hero. Why did you head over to Bull's in the first place? You can't have seriously thought it would do any good. You're just a skinny thing."

I've been thinking about this myself, tossing it around in my head. It was more than anger. There was something else pushing me through the woods that night.

I lean on the mower's handle and furrow my brow. "Have you ever had one of them notions—and it just comes up on you like a wave—that things are much worse than you thought or have been told? That maybe you're missing a clue or a warning sign that's saying, 'Hey, looky here'?" I saw a hint of recognition in his eyes. "That's what I felt, Jimmy. That's what I still feel. Trent wouldn't have just up and left like that, I don't think. He was thinking me and him had a future together. He would have hidden for a bit in the woods, then come and found me at the carnival when the coast was clear."

"You think Bull has him?"

"Or has done something to him." That thought gives me the shivers, and the shivers when you're hot is a god-awful feeling. "Anyway, that's why I went there. Things are much worse than I thought they were. You ever get that feeling, Jimmy?"

All of a sudden-like, things go shady. The sun has been hidden by big bruised clouds, blue and gray. A breeze sweeps past and around us, making us both shake of cold chills. We look up at the clouds. They're moving fast across the sky, like they're trying to get away from something.

Looking back at Jimmy, he's studying me with a worried expression. "Yes," he answers, almost in a whisper.

I look over his shoulder. Leroy is on the porch. He is standing all strange, like he's one of those wavy balloon men you see at car dealerships. The breeze is treating him just so. Jimmy's off running towards him. Leroy collapses onto the porch floor. Jimmy's yelling his name something fierce.

I take off running after Jimmy. Something's gone terribly wrong.

The wind kicks up and there's a growl of thunder.

* * * *

It's raining as Jimmy peels out of the driveway, gravel and dust flying, with Leroy slouched over in the front seat. They're headed to the hospital in Devlin. The storm they been telling us about is here, and that ain't no metaphor. I watch as the big blue Buick disappears into the haze of dust and rain. There's not much else I can do as far as yard work goes—I wouldn't be focused anyway—so I put the mower away and head on back to the carnival. My tank top is wet as hell. I slip it into the side of my jeans so that it hangs there like a do-rag. I have to keep pushing my wet hair out of my face. Leroy has offered to trim it for me.

Damn. I sure hope Leroy's okay. He's a good guy. Wait. That makes it sound like he's someone I met on the street. Leroy's my friend.

It's funny how drops of rain on leaves sounds like commiseration. I just noticed that right now. For the first time, maybe ever, I feel comforted by these woods. Everything looks the same, but there's a voice to the trees now. This walk is calming me, doing me good, and I slow down. I don't want it to end so quickly. I just want to think—or not think—and hear the trees.

I get the feeling somebody's watching me. Somebody other than the trees, that is. Looking up, I see Nessa. She's wet as I am, still in a tank and jeans and not wearing any shoes. Her hair collects the rain like a sponge. Her face is softer than I ever seen it.

"You heading to the carnival?" she asks me. She knows the answer, of course. Why'd she ask?

"Yes, ma'am." I speak above the sound of the rain on the leaves. "Headed home."

She stares at me, as if she expects me to say more. She's got a sadness to her, a real grief I ain't noticed before. Maybe because every time I've run into her it's been when I was frazzled or frightened and worried about myself.

"Leroy's sick," I say, feeling a bit uncomfortable with the awkwardness of the moment. "Real sick. Jimmy's taken him to the hospital. Do you know Jimmy and Leroy?"

"I know 'em," she says with a nod. She's staring me down, like she's stripping off my skin to look at my soul or something. "They's good folk."

"Yes, ma'am."

"It'll work out," she says, I guess trying to give me some level of comfort.

"Yes, ma'am," I say once more. "Well, I best be getting on to the carnival." I move on past her, figuring our fine conversation is finished.

"You know where to find me," she says.

"Ma'am?"

"Call me Nessa. You know where to find me, Charlie. You know where my home is here in the woods. When you're ready."

"Ready, ma'am—I mean, Nessa? For what?"

But that's all I get from her. She turns around and disappears behind a big ol' tree. And when I say disappear, that's exactly what I mean. She ain't nowhere to be seen. It's like the forest floor done opened up and swallowed her whole. Nessa knows these woods better than me. She's got shortcuts I can only dream of having.

* * * *

It feels real, but I know it's a dream. Still, I don't think to pinch myself. I'm standing in the middle of the carnival at night. All the lights are on and the rides are whirling, buzzing, and swooshing, but at a rate I ain't never seen them. They're all going too fast, as if time has sped up. The music is playing, but it sounds different because it's been fixed, tuned. The rust has been wiped away, the weeds and brush cleared, and every colored bulb is bright and new. The place looks unfamiliar to me all spruced up like this. Like I ain't supposed to be here. Like I'm an unwanted freak in this particular sideshow. Unwanted by whom, I've no idea. There still ain't a soul to be seen.

Until now.

I see a man appear. He rounds the sideshow tent corner and he's walking in slow motion, like he's in a different time-scape. It's a deliberate walk, with broad steps and swinging arms. He's wearing an old suit and a bowler hat, but I can't make out his face. He's coming straight at me, and I can't move. It would be in my best interest to move. I can feel that in my bones. But I am anchored here, rooted, petrified as he gets closer.

He stands in front of me, as tall as I am, and I can feel his breath on my face. It's ice cold. The hairs on my neck are prickly. The shadow that's been hiding his features lifts from his face, and what I see is a terrifying mess: eyes and lips twirling, whirling, grimacing, and gritting like he's been exposed to some dangerous chemical and has no control over them. Like his nerves are all fucked up. But even as his face goes wild, I can hear a deep chuckle. Not a laugh. A chuckle. And because it wants to keep me asleep, that's enough to frighten me awake.

I'm sweating in my log. The carnival music is playing outside, sounding sour and rotting, thank god for that. I'll lie here and listen until the hour passes. Maybe, I think, I am surrounded by ghosts. But that…that was a damn demon.

* * * *

When Jimmy said Leroy would be staying in the hospital in Devlin, I thought he meant the big important-looking brick building with four floors and lots of parking, the one with all the frenetic nurses and doctors walking about in their white coats, and injured or sick folk in the hallways all convinced their lives were coming to an end. Instead, he gave me directions to a little out-of-the-way structure on the outskirts of town in what could be described as the "ghetto" district of Devlin. This is where the poorest of the poor live. I say that knowing that these folk are still wealthier than me. They at least have televisions. I haven't seen a television in years. Jimmy and Leroy don't even own a television, but that's just because they don't want one. "It's a drain on the brain," says Jimmy, "not to mention resources."

The structure I arrive at is a free clinic. I have discovered this bit of information thanks to a kind but exhausted secretary named Florence, and it's where sick people come who haven't got any insurance and can't afford to go to the big hospital. I had no idea this place existed. It's something to keep in mind if I ever get sick. Maybe I should have them look at that dog bite on my thigh. Leroy did a fine job, of course, but it wouldn't hurt to get a second opinion, right?

I'm being led by Florence through a hallway chock-full with sick or bleeding people, each one of them looking up at me like I'm cutting in line. "Ain't no thing," I wanna tell them. "Just here to visit a friend." I don't think they'd care one way or the other. They're just looking for somewhere to place their anger, someone to blame for their lot in life. Everybody's dying here.

The room is so small and so crammed full of electronic doctor stuff it makes me claustrophobic. Leroy's hooked up to a heart monitor that, even to my untrained eyes, looks out-of-date. It beeps too loudly. Jimmy is sitting in a chair beside Leroy, reading a magazine on spoiled movie stars and their spoiled lives. Must be a good article, because he don't notice me until Florence croaks out "You've got visitors," then leaves.

Leroy, who looked to be almost asleep, brightens right up when he sees me. I got to say, it's wonderful to have that effect on someone. It's like I almost have purpose. His still handsome face stretches with a smile. "Well, look who it is, Jimmy!" says Leroy, his voice sounding too heavy for his body. "It's our boy, Charlie. Come on over here, Charlie, and give me a hug."

I squeeze past all the doctor stuff and do as I'm told. Leroy feels light in my embrace, like his strength is leaking from him. He's got all kinds of pins and needles stuck in his arms.

"How you feeling, Leroy?" I ask. "Gonna be going home soon?"

"You better believe it," he says. "I'm just in here for a pit stop. Just need some refuelin' is all. It happens every so often. I overstress myself."

I look to Jimmy. His eyes tell me that ain't exactly so. "He'll be up and fixin' us breakfast again in no time," he says anyway. "And I can't wait. The food here in town is just plain awful. What the hell is a McRueben? Can somebody please explain the thought process that goes into creatin' somethin' like that? It's a damn travesty."

"At least you get a break from that, huh?" I say to Leroy. "From cooking all the time."

"I don't mind cookin'," he says. "Fact is, I love it. It keeps my mind off how tired I am." He looks real sad for a moment, like Fate's just told him his future, whispered it right in his ear. Sometimes I wish I could get into someone's head, you know? Just to know what they're thinking.

"You okay, Leroy?" asks Jimmy, reaching for Leroy's hand. "Want me to get the doctor?"

"I'm fine. Just tired, is all. Just real damn tired. Ain't nothin' makes a person more tired than layin' down all day. It zaps your strength and your will." He looks into Jimmy's eyes. "I was young and healthy once, you know."

"I know," says Jimmy. Jimmy's eyes are getting watery.

"I was." He says it like a reaffirmation to himself, even as he looks to be dozing off.

"Come on, Charlie," says Jimmy. "Let's give Princess Leroy some time for his beauty sleep. I'll buy you a McRueben."

"Fuck you," says Leroy, but he smiles as he closes his eyes.

We're out in the hall, and I swear I nearly see Jimmy break down. He bows his head, one hand outstretched against the wall, and swallows hard.

"If you need to cry," I say, "there ain't no shame in it."

He looks up to me with glassy eyes. "Ain't you somethin'?" he says and sniffs. "We'll get ol' Leroy better and back home. Don't you worry none about that. But things are gonna be different. I'm gonna be the one takin' care of him now. I'll be doin' the cookin'."

"I imagine Leroy will have something to say about that."

"I imagine he will too," says Jimmy. "Yessir. I imagine he will have quite a bit to say on that subject. I can't cook a fried egg."

"You gonna teach yourself?"

"I'm gonna do my best, Charlie boy." He wipes his eyes with his hands. "Now, let's find you a doctor to look at that dog bite. I want to be able to tell Leroy what a great job he did fixin' you up when he wakes, that even the doctor said so."

* * * *

I'm let into the townhouse once again by Patricia's handsome nurse. He looks at me with indifference when he opens the door, still doesn't say a word, and he leads me down the long dark hallway to her room. He ain't dressed like a nurse. Certainly not like those I saw at the free clinic. This fella's dressed in a suit, like he might be headed to a business meeting somewhere after he's done seeing to Patricia. I'd ask his name, but I don't think he'd reply. He probably thinks I'm beneath him. Most folk do. Most folk are right, I guess.

I hear a violin being played. It's echoing through the large, murky townhouse like it's coming from someone's memory. It's real pretty, though. Being self-educated, I'm not too familiar with music. I've spent most of my time reading about other things, and I've never even picked up an instrument. But I know pretty music when I hear it. That said, there's a strangeness to the playing. Like it's just a bit too fast. It's a bit eerie. Even quick things can creep.

I'm led past a wall—rows upon rows, reaching all the way up to the ceiling—of fractured crystal. I've passed it before, of course, but paid no mind to it. I've always just come here to do Patricia and then I leave. It's a job, after all. This time, however, the music makes me actually slow down and look at the collection on the wall. Vases, goblets, animal figurines, windmills, all sorts of pretty crystal and blown glass refracting the dim light, and every one of them broken somehow and glued back together. There ain't a perfect piece among them. It's almost as if that is the point of the whole collection. Like that was their purpose, you know, to be nearly perfect but clearly flawed.

The nurse stands to the side as I enter Patricia's bedchamber. I think I hear him take a deep breath at my passing, like he's gonna say something, but I can't be sure. Patricia is on the bed as usual, in a similar black gown to last time. Her attention is focused on a man who is standing in front of her playing the violin. I stay by the door until I'm invited to the bed. The bedchamber seems more dimly lit today. There's four of us in the room now, soaking up the light. The violinist is a huge man. He's in his forties, maybe fifties, already bald but for a swath of brown hair around his ears. He's got a thin nose and is wearing delicate-looking glasses. His head seems too small for the rest of his body, like someone's switched doll parts. He wears a tuxedo, and that doesn't seem right on him either. Clearly, this man is a bodybuilder or a strong man. This seems a warring contradiction to me. Muscle and music. Masculine and feminine.

Patricia finally notices me and holds up her hand. The violinist stops playing immediately. "Charlie," Patricia says to me, her face almost expressing a smile. "This is Carter. You, of course, already know Orlando, my nurse." I look back at the doorway where the nurse still stands. He still seems indifferent. "Come sit with me, Charlie."

I take off my shoes and climb up next to her. She pulls up a pillow, and I sit in her arms against the headboard. The scent of lilacs in this room is overpowering. It always has been, like she's going to great lengths to cover some putrid smell. She gestures for Carter to continue playing, and the pretty but slightly too quick music begins again.

"Do you know this piece?" she asks me, whispering in my ear.

"No, ma'am," I answer.

"Of course not." The tone of knowing condescension in her voice is grating. "Well, it's a violin concerto. Violin concertos are all about love. It's disgusting. This one in particular is about butterflies in love. A silly notion, don't you think? Those creatures are delicate enough. They don't need to worry about being torn to pieces by love. I abhor violin concertos."

"But then, why are you listening to it?"

"Because I love irony. Ironic, isn't it? That I love irony. Now hush and let's be ironic together."

I don't know how to be ironic. It sounds like an ugly, mean thing to me. But she pays me to pretend all the time, so I guess this ain't no different than pretending to be attracted to her. In truth, I find the music playful at times and lulling at others. It's nice and it puts me in a real relaxed zone, like somebody's spilt roofies in the air. I'm damn comfortable but for the spindly arms around my shoulder that feel like a steel bar keeping me locked on a carnival ride.

I think Patricia notices my comfort, my relaxation, because she says, "It's tricked you, this music."

"Ma'am?" I ask, slightly irritated to be pulled out of my tranquil state.

"The music is in your soul, lying to you, telling you love is wonderful." She puts a finger on my chin and gently turns my head towards her. "It's not real." She kisses me on the mouth. It's long and delicate, but there ain't no emotion behind it. "It's not real," she repeats. "It's just chemicals and hormones. Tiny little biological actors working together to fool you."

"Maybe it's a little real?" I say.

"Orlando," she calls for her nurse over the music. He's at the bedside faster than I can turn my head. "Kiss our guest. Show him how real love is."

Orlando doesn't hesitate. He bends over the bed and plants a kiss, just as passionless as Patricia's, on my lips. Then he stands up straight again and walks back to his station by the door.

"Do you see?" Patricia says with a wicked smile. "Nothing. No love at all. Orlando couldn't care if you lived or died, Charlie. Most people don't. I admit, seeing such lovely young men kiss one another is very erotic, but any idea that the two of you or even you and I will go off and have a happy life together is sheer fantasy on my part. After you are through with me tonight, dear Charlie, you will go back to wherever you came from, most likely service some other person in some vile and revolting way, and Orlando here will get my water ready for my bath."

"So, love is what?" The violinist continues playing, though at a slower pace.

I must have hit a nerve, because she starts talking much louder. "There's certainly nothing supernatural about it. It's just a way evolution came up with to trick us into thinking there's something deeper associated with our purpose on this planet, to make us feel connected so the species can survive. We use each other for pleasure or procreation, and we call it love." She pauses. "Now, shall we get down to business?"

This stays in my head even as I'm servicing Patricia, even as she has me service Orlando for her amusement and his humiliation, even as Carter plays the violin over it all. Finally, and not a minute too soon, as they say, the night is over and Orlando sees me out without even so much as a "thank you for the blowjob." Ah well. I don't think he enjoyed it anyway. The boy looks lobotomized.

I'm halfway down the block, heading back to the carnival before it gets dark, and I hear my name called. "Charlie!" It sounded like a thump. Dumb-sounding, like something thrown in the bottom of a big plastic tub. I turn to see Carter, the muscle-man violinist, jogging towards me in his tux with his violin case in hand. If Patricia wants me to come back, I'm gonna run.

"Don't believe her," he says to me, a little out of breath. I don't guess fellas his size do a lot of running. "Don't believe her, what she said about love. It ain't true, Charlie. Love is real. Love is a real thing, and it's got just as much to do with the supernatural as the biological."

"I have suspected as much," I reply.

"Good," says Carter. "But it is dangerous. Ain't no lie in that. You fall in love and…well, just read your Shakespeare."

He stands there, awkward-like, waiting for me to say something, I guess. My thumbs are in my pants pockets, an affectation I find that helps me get clients.

It works. He whispers, "What are your rates, Charlie?"

I give him a grin. Mr. Carter's looking for love. "Tell you what," I say, leaning on one foot. "Since you been so nice to me and chased me down to make sure I'm okay, I'll cut you a deal. Half price. That's ten dollars for an hour. How's that sound, sir?"

I can see it now. Yessir. I got myself a new client. I can tell by that gleam in his eyes.

* * * *

I've been helping Jimmy move things around in the old caretaker's house. Leroy is home, and Jimmy is as happy as a momma hen. The day before Leroy left the clinic we moved the bed here, downstairs into this gray ghost parlor. The bed is huge, so that weren't no easy feat for just two fellas. Jimmy even moved some of the other bedroom furnishings—what little there is—into the parlor so it doesn't seem so blah and uninhabitable. I found an old painting in the haunted house at the carnival—a portrait of a pretty girl—and hung it in one of the empty spaces on the wall. It ain't really their cup of tea—pretty girls, that is—but Jimmy said it livened up the place. He was real pleased. Jimmy plans to live downstairs now too. The doc told him that Leroy needs some space to recover, but Jimmy thinks that's bullshit and told the doc so. A fella needs to be held tight when he's as sick as Leroy is, or so Jimmy thinks.

"I don't want his ornery soul escaping from his body," he said. "Not without me tagging along after."

I'm standing in the middle of the parlor as Jimmy helps Leroy out of the Buick and into the house. Leroy is struggling, breathing hard, but his face lights up at once when he sees me. Jimmy helps him give me a hug. I lead the way inside. Leroy does a double take when he sees the room.

"Why, you outdid yourselves," he says, his weakened voice trying hard to augment his delight. "Jimmy told me you was changin' things around, but…damn! I never expected this."

I help get Leroy into bed. He's tired from the excitement of the day—leaving the clinic, the drive home, and the walk into the house—but I can see from his face that he's damn pleased to be home, sleeping in his own bedsheets. His breathing is labored as we get him situated and wrapped up in an old blanket.

"It's not even midafternoon," Leroy says in his deep but exhausted voice, "and here I am in bed. Pathetic."

"Hush your mouth," says Jimmy. "The doc says you're to get lots of rest. I don't agree with him on everything, but I agree with that. I'm your nurse, and I'll be doin' the cleanin' and cookin' around here. When you need to head to the bathroom, you just tell me and we'll get it done right quick. It's my turn to take care of you."

"Well, that's it, then, Charlie," mutters Leroy. "I'm as good as dead."

"Don't worry, Leroy," I say. "I'll be helping out as much as I can. If you need anything, just ask."

Leroy looks to Jimmy. "Ain't he somethin'?"

"He sure is," says Jimmy. "And don't think I won't be workin' you hard when you're here, Charlie. If you're offerin' to help, well, I'm gonna take you serious."

"Charlie boy, do not let him go out on that porch with a glass of iced tea. It's the last you'll see of him."

"Huh," says Jimmy. "Nurse Jimmy ain't leavin' your side, you wretched showman. Not ever. And don't you leave mine." Jimmy bends down and kisses Leroy gently on the lips. It makes me smile. It makes both of them smile too. I look out the bay window so they can have a moment. "Now," Jimmy says after kissy-face is over, "what do you want to eat? I know you're hungry. I've been hearin' your tummy bitchin' and moanin' all the way home. You didn't eat much at the clinic at all."

"Do ya blame me?"

"No, I do not. So. What do you want?"

"If you can manage it," says Leroy, "I'd love some eggs and toast."

"Shit. I can do that. I practiced my egg-cookin' yesterday afternoon, didn't I, Charlie? I'll be back in a jiffy."

"Well, then I won't be eatin' it because you can't make good eggs and toast in a jiffy."

"Huh," says Jimmy as he heads into the kitchen.

I sit down in an old wooden chair next to the bed. Leroy closes his eyes and lies back against the headboard. He holds up a finger as if he don't want me to speak, as if he's waiting for an answer from Jimmy to a question that wasn't ever asked in the first place. The heat is oppressive, and there's an annoying fly in the parlor with us. From the kitchen, I hear the sizzle of grease in the frying pan and the even more excited sizzle of bacon. Leroy smiles and opens his eyes.

"He's makin' bacon," he says. "I didn't ask for it, but damn, I wanted it. He knows me by heart. I love the sound of food cookin': the sizzlin', the fryin', the boilin', the bakin'. It's like music to my ears, Charlie. Combined with the smells, it's like a goddamned symphony." He looks at me. "Do you like music, Charlie boy?"

I think of two o'clock in the morning at the carnival. I think of Carter and his violin. And I think of Patricia and her irony. "What I've heard of it, yessir. I do."

"I heard someone say once that music is the language of love. That may be the silliest thing I've ever heard. But it might be true too. A cliché is a cliché for a reason. Because as I said, right now, with Jimmy in there cookin' for me, that's music to my ears. And that's love, Charlie."

"Yessir," I say. "I believe you."

* * * *

Jimmy wants me to stay at the caretaker's house tonight with him and Leroy. He hates the thought of me all alone in the carnival, especially after all the help I've been. Leroy's done nodded off to sleep after finishing the meal Jimmy made him. He complained about most of it, but Jimmy didn't fail to point out that "you finished it, didn't ya?"

As I'm leaving, Jimmy stands with me for a moment out on the porch. "You sure I can't persuade you to stay?" he asks. It's dusk now, and the woods are already gonna be darker than dark on my way home, so there's no use hurrying. "I've noticed some tire tracks on our property. Big thick overcompensatin' tires. Bull's been about. He's watchin' for ya, Charlie boy."

"Bull can't catch me." I say it, but I don't believe it.

"What do ya mean he can't catch ya? He's already done it once."

"I was caught off guard, that was all," I say. "I got my eyes open now. I know what to look for, what to listen for."

"I suppose a dog bite will do that."

"Yessir." I descend the porch steps and start my walk back to the carnival. "Tell Leroy I said goodnight. I hope he feels all kinds of better tomorrow."

"Will do. You keep yourself safe, Charlie boy."

"Will do."

The katydids are gossiping tonight like I ain't never heard. It's enough to make a man go deaf. There ain't nothing but them to be heard. I kick the gravel beneath my feet, but keep my eyes focused straight ahead. The days here seem to get longer as the summer goes on, longer and hotter and more spiteful. There's still some light in the sky, though in these woods you wouldn't know it. The trees like it dark here. I wipe the sweat from my brow and notice something shiny up ahead, just on the side of the road. I squint, stare harder, and then stop. I realize what it is—who it is—and dive into the woods. The growl from the engine gives the truck away even without the glare from the headlights. If Bull thinks he's being stealthy, he's a damn fool. Katydids ain't no match for a monster truck.

I stay still, crouched behind a briar bush, and watch as the snarling truck slowly backs off, turns, and then drives away blind. It's so loud, even from the distance and beneath the chorus of katydids, Jimmy is bound to have heard it. This is all gonna come to no good. I can feel it. Jimmy and Leroy got guns, but they're gonna need a whole lot more firepower than that to get rid of that truck. It's gonna take the devil out of hell.

I stay crouched where I am for a bit more, just to be safe, just to make sure Bull isn't coming back. You can never be too safe. Not when it comes to that bastard. I don't want Bull following me back to the carnival. What would he do if he ever found out I lived there?

* * * *

I'm dreaming of the carnival again. There's no well-dressed man with a messed-up face this time, though. No, thank god for that. I'm seated at a show in a bright red tent, and all around me are people, an audience, every one of them with frozen smiles on their faces. Expectation, maybe. But I notice something that makes me uneasy. It ain't just their exaggerated smiles that are frozen. Not a single one of them spectators is moving but me. Hands are stopped just short of applauding, and there ain't even a blinking eye among them. And that sound I hear ain't the rush of gasping or awe from wonderstruck onlookers. It's the breath of silence, cold, waiting silence. I touch the man next to me—a tall man with a long face stretched into an uncomfortable grin—but he doesn't respond. He feels hollow, as does his expression of excitement, like it's been put on. Painted on. Fixed. This man's a mannequin like those in the haunted house. As much as his skin feels like flesh, he ain't real.

But those men in the ring are real. I breathe a sigh of relief. Familiarity at last. That's Leroy and Jimmy. They look prime and healthy, though. Even Leroy. He looks like he could lift a horse, arms bulging, muscles striating. They're both in skintight white sequined costumes, displaying feats of strength, Leroy holding Jimmy at strange angles with only a hand and Jimmy trusting him to do so. It's effortless. They're not showing any signs of fatigue or struggle. It's fluid and easy and beautiful as a dance. I'm smiling. I'm sure I'm smiling. I want to shout at them, to make sure they know I'm here. But then I realize, this ain't me.

I look at my hands, a slightly gaudy thumb ring gleaming back at me from a fleshier digit, and I know that I'm no longer Charlie. I'm Trent, and I'm wondering what the hell I've gotten myself into.

It's all gone dark suddenly. I look up, and the tent is gone. So are the mannequins and Jimmy and Leroy. The silent spectators are replaced by silent katydids. They're there, though, watching me from behind the rocks and trees of this dark forest that feels even more perilous and unfamiliar to me than usual. And now, by god, this don't feel like a dream no more. I get the for-certain feeling that this is a memory, but it ain't mine. This belongs to Trent.

I have the urge to scream, to run, and so I do. I'm tripping over branches and logs and big ol' rocks that I—as in Charlie—I know are there. But Trent doesn't. He don't know these woods like me. He's so fucking scared. *What's he scared of?* I wonder. *What's making his heart beat so fast I can feel it in my ears?* He's screaming my name. Screaming for "Charlie! Charlie!" and I want to help him. I want to be right there and show him the way out. My god, he's terrified. I'm terrified.

I hear it now. I hear the dog, and I hear Bull. I know what's happening. This is the night Trent disappeared. This is the night we were separated. Suddenly, I don't want to know what happens to him. I don't want to be there, because what can I do about it now? I separate from him. I am an observer, not a participant in this dream memory. I want to close my eyes, because whatever is gonna happen can't be good. Trent's cries for help are already breaking my heart.

He trips as he's running, and I want to cry out to him to get up, but it's too late. The dog is on top of him, and he's screaming for me still. The dog is biting him, tearing his flesh, showing no mercy.

And there's Bull, standing over Trent with a big grin on his face, saying, "Good dog, good dog."

Now we're in the swamp by Bull's house, his slapped-together shack. The dog is growling, Bull is smirking, and Trent is tied to a stump. He's whimpering and bloody, pleading with Bull to let him go, swearing that he won't ever come to these woods again. He's wet, soaking, but that ain't water. It's petrol. Pure gasoline. Oh fuck, no! No, no, no, no. Bull's eyes are dark pits without a hint of humanity. I catch my breath as Bull lights a match and throws it. The swamp is suddenly bright with an angry orange light. Trent's screams, his cries for me, reach blistering proportions as he burns. The fire roars as it engulfs him, and the dog barks, and Bull stares with a widening grin on his face.

But Trent screams, "Charlie! Oh god, Charlie!"

I wake up screaming and in tears. The log I'm sleeping in rocks a little on its tracks, then steadies, but I continue to shake. That image…Trent, the flames dancing in his hair, over his face. Jesus Christ! He was crying for me but I never heard. I was probably already back here lying safe in this very log. What would possess a man to burn someone alive? What would possess a man? I can't breathe. I wish I was dead.

The carnival music is playing outside. My head falls back down on my makeshift pillow, and I cry. *I was never your hero, Trent. Godammit! I was never your hero.*

* * * *

Leroy is always teasing Jimmy about being lazy, about not helping out, but that ain't really so. Jimmy just likes to do things in his own time, is all. He don't see a point to being rushed. Even when he was teaching, he liked to give his students extra time to finish their reports. He's sweet iced tea on a summer's day. Anyone who believes what Leroy says, thinking it's anything but a jibe, only has to look out the back door. There's a big garden filled with almost every kind of vegetable known to man, all grown by Jimmy just for Leroy to cook with. Jimmy may be an awful cook, but he's got a thumb as green as a wet frog. The garden is near a noisy chicken coop and is as overgrown and wild as the front yard was before I mowed it. There are giant stalks of golden corn, big ol' squashes, and juicy tomatoes, cabbage and lettuce and cauliflower, and rows and rows of beans, both green and otherwise. There's even a nice line of pretty flowers climbing up yardsticks, all of them bright purple or red. Jimmy walks through it today like he's surveying his kingdom. These days he does that surveying with a little less haught, though. His mind is occupied, like the front parlor, by Leroy.

I'm helping pick some beans, dropping them into a plastic peanut butter container with a dull thump. Jimmy wants to try out Leroy's green bean casserole tonight. I'm doing my best to keep my mind off the nightmare I had last night, off Trent's memory. If I don't, I will surely break down and cry. But that image of Trent's hair curling in the flames…

"How is Leroy?" I ask Jimmy. Spoken words are the best method for shutting up inner thoughts. "He doing better?"

My question seems to wake Jimmy from his own distressed stupor. He looks up at me as if he done forgot I was there. A gentleness comes back into his eyes, replacing a cold detachment I don't recognize in him.

"I think he's good," says Jimmy. "I think he's…better."

I think he's lying.

"Well, that's good," I say, awkwardness rolling off my tongue like tree sap. I never heard Jimmy lie before. He doesn't do it very well.

"You can go on home, Charlie," Jimmy says after a minute. "I think you got enough there."

This is the first time I recall ever being asked to leave the caretaker's house by Jimmy.

"Are you sure, Jimmy? I can stay and—"

"Just go." The look in his eyes is one of irritation.

I don't argue. I just stand and avoid eye contact.

"Sure, Jimmy," I say. "I'll put these in the kitchen."

I'm not asked back for dinner tonight. I'm relieved about that.

I look in on Leroy as I pass through the parlor on my way out. He's fast asleep and slowly dying. I hate to say that, but it's the plain truth. In many ways, he's the strongest man I ever met. In others…well, you just have to look at him.

I'm standing here for too long. I realize this when he opens his eyes and sees me. I hope he don't see my pity.

"You leavin', Charlie boy?" he asks, a smile struggling to form on his face. "Don't I deserve a goodbye?"

"Aw, sure you do," I say, walking nearer to the bed. "I just didn't want to wake you, Leroy. You looked all peaceful. You need your sleep. Doctor says so. Jimmy says so."

"Everybody says so. But you know, the more sleep I get, the more tired I feel. I guess that's what they call a double-edged sword." He squints at me. "And you look like you need a good week's worth of rest yourself, boy. You been out partyin' all night? Got yourself a girl or a fella?"

"I ain't never been to a party. Not a proper one, anyway. And I ain't never had a girlfriend…or a boyfriend."

"That just means ain't nobody been worthy of you yet." Leroy pats the bed. "Come here and sit down," he says. "Tell me what's on your mind."

I look back in the direction of Jimmy and the garden.

"Don't worry none about him," says Leroy. "He's been in a mood all day. Now, come on. Sit down."

I'm careful not to sit down too forcefully. I don't want to jar anything loose in Leroy, if that's possible.

"What's botherin' you, Charlie boy?" asks Leroy. "Tell me a story."

I don't want to add to his worries, especially with something so bizarre and maybe not even real. "I'm…I'm just tired," I lie. I'll be dishonest with you: I'm a better liar than Jimmy.

"You are tired. Yes, indeed. Anyone can see it. But there's a reason for your lack of sleep, ain't there?" He coughs something awful up, his convulsions shaking the room, and spits it in the trash can at the side of the bed. "Spill it," he says once he's regained his composure.

"How can you be so sure there's something on my mind?"

"Because, Charlie boy, you've got a poet's heart and your face is a book, plain as day."

I sincerely hope Jimmy stays in the garden. "I had a dream last night," I say. "Only it wasn't a dream. It was like…like a memory, but not mine. Understand?"

I doubt he does. He's listening just the same, though. His eyes are tired and ringed, but open.

I go on, but in a softer tone. "It was Trent's memory. I know that sounds crazy, but as sure as I'm here talking to you, I felt I was watching, even being, Trent. And Leroy, I was terrified. It was a memory of that night. The night he went missing after Bull came after us, the night I was chased through the woods. I was hoping against hope, even praying, that Trent got away, but I know now that ain't so. That ain't so."

I wipe away a tear and try to hide my face by turning it.

I take a deep breath. "I saw Bull tie Trent up to a tree stump there in his swamp. He soaked him in petrol and then lit a match. Trent screamed and screamed as he burned. He screamed for me, he screamed my name. But Leroy, I never heard him. Not one cry. I was safe inside the carnival. I swear I never heard a single cry for help."

Leroy swallows. I suck in my breath and wipe my nose. I almost didn't make it through the telling.

"What do you think it means?" I ask. I don't truly expect Leroy to know the answer, but I ask anyway. "Was it a true memory?"

"Sometimes," says Leroy, not lifting his gaze from me, "when Jimmy is asleep and I wake up in the middle of the night, when everything is as dark as black velvet, I swear there are others here in the house with us. Not people so much as…"

"The grays?"

He nods. "I've seen them for a while now, Charlie. Even before I got sick. They don't do anything, and at first I was tempted—willin'—to think that Jimmy was right. That they were nothin' more than plays of light or fever dreams. But they were such specific plays of light. And then Jimmy saw 'em too, though he don't remember it, when he was high and went on that shootin' spree." Leroy pauses and looks out the bay window. "I woke up last night. Jimmy was here, snorin' next to me as always, the useless bum, and I saw three of them. The grays, that is. They were standin' where you was a few minutes ago. Just standin' there, watchin' me. Gray folk with discernible arms and legs, one of 'em near as tall as the room, and they was swayin' a bit back and forth but not movin' towards me. Just standin' there. Regardin' me."

"Sweet Jesus," I whisper. I feel the chills creep down my back. The room feels suddenly much cooler.

"What are they, Charlie?" Leroy looks back at me. "What do they mean? If you can tell me that, I'll sure as hell try to answer your question."

And I see it. Leroy is just as scared as I am.

* * * *

Nessa's shack is hard to find, but after leaving Leroy alone so he could sleep, I've come to find her, thinking she might be able to help me figure some things out. Rumors are rumors, and most of them are lies, but there's always a seed of truth that gets them started. I can't even remember who first put the notion in my head that Nessa was a witch. Maybe I made it up myself. It's not like I know anyone else who's even been in these woods.

It's midafternoon. The birds are cawing; the katydids are trilling. Finding her shack was easier than I thought. Nessa's seated on the edge of her porch, whittling away at a big tree branch with a small knife. Looks like she's making a spear. She sees me but keeps on working. I stay where I am. It's bad manners to approach someone, to steal into their space, without being asked first. Don't need to be taught it to know it.

"Been expectin' you," she says. "You sure do take your time."

Not much to say about the shack. There's a big ol' cooking pot sitting on kindling out in front, but that's about it. That's her witch's cauldron, I suppose. Everything else is green leaves and thistles, tall trees and briars.

I give some distance between us as I sit down on the edge of the porch too. It's a small knife she holds, sure, but that's a big spear she's making, and I ain't ever handled neither.

"Don't worry none," she says. "It's for huntin' and that's all. For now, anyway. Now, what you wanna ask me?"

I swallow and tell her what I just told Leroy, down to the letter. I don't get quite as emotional this time, though.

"Is he dead, Miss Nessa?" I ask her. "Is Trent dead?"

She continues sharpening her spear. "Yeah. He dead. But you knew that, Charlie. You didn't need me to answer you that. Is that all you came for?" She puts down the spear and the knife and looks at me all disappointed-like. "I ain't some wise woman who lives in the woods, boy. You got some mythology built around me, don't ya? Like I'm a witch or sorceress who can bring your friend back to life. Well, that ain't me, boy. You been readin' too many books. I ain't sayin' those type of people don't exist, but I ain't one of them. I wouldn't wanna be. I can hear the dead sometimes, when they wanna be heard. Some of 'em do an awful lot of talkin'. But that's it."

She picks up her spear again and starts working like we was done talking. I sit there, stunned by the truth I already knew was so. I think I just needed to hear it from somebody else. My delicate friend Trent was murdered, set afire like a piece of paper.

* * * *

"Your friend," she says, maybe seeing I am not taking her assurances all that well, "he better now. He not in any pain anymore. He wanted you to know that. But he forgettin' things now, honey."

"Forgetting things?"

"Forgettin' this life. Every bit of it," she says. "It's as natural as learnin' somethin' new. You see, when we die, every one of us become a spirit. Ghosts. Haunts. Whatever you wanna call it. We shed our bodies, and we just float alongside the elementals. We stay spirits until we bleed out all of our memories from this life. It can be a long process, sure. Some folk have stronger attachments and memories than others. Some folk have deeper hurts and more egregious anger, so they stick around for a longer time. Some never leave. In time, they forget who or even what they was. They fumble about in an endless shade of gray, forgettin' why they were angry in the first place but holdin' on to that anger tight just the same." She looks me square in the face. "But that wasn't your friend. You should know that. Maybe it'll help you sleep better, yes? He was not an angry soul, honey. He's gone on."

"To where?" I wanna cry again.

She shrugs. "Who knows, hon? He could be off in the Evermore now, the land of Heaven. Or maybe he already been reincarnated. Maybe he a little girl who just been born in India. Maybe he a prince. Maybe he waitin' to return later, years and years from now. The point his, he ain't in any pain and his last thoughts as he met Death was of you."

"Death?"

"Mhmm. Death is a soul, as real as me or you."

"Was he scared, do you think?" I ask. "Meeting Death, I mean."

"Probably, boy. Wouldn't you be? I know I'm scared to meet him, and I've been in this world lots longer than you. But from what I understand, from what been passed to me, when Death comes to us, he greets us disguised as the last person we knew and loved who has died, I suppose for comfort's sake, if you can get past the whole dyin' thing."

"How do you know all this, Miss Nessa?" I ask.

She shrugs again. "Just bits of what I been able to glean. Other bits my momma told me when I was a girl." She examines her spear, seemingly happy with her work. There's no smile, but there is a slight nod of approval. That thing could shish kebab an elephant. "Momma and my brother Ray, they worked some years ago at that ol' carnival you call home. Momma was the fortune teller, though she had real talent in the sorcerer's arts. Truth be told, that carnival was a waste of what god gave her. She coulda helped people, maybe even the police, with her gift, but people got to make a livin'. Ray, he was a groundskeeper. He was a big strong fella. Mhmm. The ladies were wild about Ray. Momma liked workin' at the carnival fine enough, though she never cared much for the caretaker. She said he was surrounded by darkness. His darkness, she said, was growin'. One day, me and her, we leave. She said the caretaker was lookin' to do us harm. We move off and find another gig, this time at a travelin' carnival. Momma couldn't convince Ray to leave, though. Naw. He was stubborn. Said he'd miss us, but that he could look after himself."

I see a deep sadness come over Nessa's face. I have to look away. It seems the right thing to do.

"When Momma died years later from cancer, I came back here with my meager savings to find my brother Ray. We hadn't heard from him since we left. Not one letter or phone call. But when I got here, he was gone. The carnival had long since closed by then. I didn't know it. I thought maybe he just moved on, found himself another gig. I was hopin' it was so, anyway."

"It wasn't so, was it?" I breathed the question out, barely speaking.

She stares at me a moment, then shakes her head. "Trust your dreams, boy. Them's your soul talkin' to ya."

I figure we are done talking so I rise to leave. She's shaken me to my core. Quick-like, though, she grabs me by the wrist. It gives my heart a start because she still has that spear and the knife. "Get yourself a glamour, Charlie," she says to me, her eyes scorching into me.

"A glamour?" I ask.

"There's a reason why that bully with the truck don't bother me. He can't see me, don't notice me. I got a glamour. Covers me and my place. I learned it from my momma."

"Can a glamour cover the carnival?"

She shakes her head slowly. "No, boy. Ain't a glamour big enough to cover that troubled place. You're gonna have to leave it, find another home, if you wanna be safe. That man, he filled with dark and dread, and he got it in for you. I see him trollin' the woods at night."

"I can't leave the carnival," I say. "It's all I know."

"You're a fool," she says, letting go of my wrist. "Ain't nobody in this world gonna give two shits about a missing runaway prostitute. When you wise up, come back to me. I'll give you a glamour."

* * * *

Walking back through the woods to the carnival, I feel watched. Like it's not just the trees that's keeping their eyes on me, it's not Nessa either, it's someone else. And there's only one other someone in these parts. If Bull's tracking me, I'm already got, glamour or no. Ain't no use in hiding now. So for once, I don't enter the carnival through the torn fence. No, I go on in through the castle gate. Like a king. Or a fool.

Part 2

I don't remember when I died, but I remember how. That is to say, I don't know the exact moment I let go of my body. I do know it was a week or so after my conversation with Nessa outside her shack in the woods, a conversation that was stinking full of omens and warnings if I had just paid attention. But then, what's that everyone always says about hindsight? I didn't speak to Jimmy or Leroy for that entire last week of my life, not even visiting the caretaker's home once. I was still concerned for Leroy, of course, but I got the feeling that Jimmy didn't want me around no more for some reason. So I just stuck to my carnival, not even watching out for Bull. Watching out for him was getting old and tired real fast. When I came and went, I used the castle gate. And I had a good run of business in Devlin all that last week.

The night I died I was with Carter the violinist. I guess, somewhere deep inside, I always knew I was gonna die young. But when you're a runaway, when you're an outcast, the future isn't ever really on your mind. Nothing beyond the next meal anyway. Certainly nothing beyond the next day. The future is always unattainable, unfathomable even. It's too far ahead to see, so why bother looking. Still, when it happened, my death, it was a bit of a shock.

* * * *

Carter is a very violent trick. He doesn't look it. By his very demeanor you'd think he was a teddy bear. But the man had—has—issues. He gets his aggression and grievances out through hard rough sex, and all that testosterone from his workouts has gotta go somewhere. I'd had a few fellas like him before, but he was the largest of them, so I was a bit anxious when things started getting more dangerous. I don't think he even knows what a safeword is.

His small apartment near Devlin's ghetto is about as big as a shoebox and smells like a used jockstrap. He shares it with musical instruments and their cases, workout equipment, and protein powders. The walls are a dirty tan and haven't been cleaned in years. Same's true for the floor. Carter was nice at first, offering me a drink and trying some nervous chitchat, but I never drank on the job and I'm not very good at talking just to talk. He downed a couple of vodka shots, and my last night on earth began. Well, my last night in a body, anyway.

He picked me up and carried me to his bed near the window. That was the first surprise. I could tell by the way he threw me onto the bed, my head hitting the wall, that he was looking for something chancy. He stiffened right up at my dazed reaction. Looking back on it, I should have left right then. But then, there's that hindsight thing again. When you're dead, everything is about looking back. I see things now like it's all just slipping away. I'm a spectator of things in which I am also an active participant. Or was. Everything is secondhand; even when it's happening, it's all past-tense and there ain't nothing can be done about it.

Before I knew it, Carter had his unsheathed dick buried deep inside my ass and a leather belt wrapped tight around my neck. I don't think he meant to kill me. He just gets off on that sort of play, on the excitement of all that control. But I flailed and I struggled and my eyes felt like they was gonna pop out of my head. I clawed at the belt, at him, but that only encouraged him. All I could hear was him grunting and growling and cursing up a storm as he drove deeper and faster into me. And that belt tightened.

And then I forgot all about him. I forgot, believe it or not, what he was doing to my body, I forgot the pain, and I no longer struggled because he was no longer there to struggle with. Somehow I was alone back in the woods. It was night, but not so dark I couldn't see the trees. Yet the forest looked different, like it'd been dipped in a dream. The trees had a silvery glow about them, like their bark was soaking wet and being hit by moonlight, only it didn't seem to have rained. More than ever, I felt the trees watching me. I could hear the bugs, the katydids and such, but they wasn't too loud, like I was hearing them through a tunnel or a sieve. Like we was in two different worlds. Everything in the forest looked and sounded fresh. Everything had a new baby smell. I wandered around in a circle, not understanding why I was suddenly there and not being fucked by Carter. And then I stopped in my circular dance. I seen a figure in front of me, and that, more than the watching trees, made me nervous. It wasn't facing me, this figure, but I recognized its shape and form.

"Trent!" I yelled, but my voice sounded just as strained as the katydids. "Trent, it's me, Charlie."

He was alive after all. Nessa was wrong.

And it was Trent. Or, at least, it was someone who looked a lot like him. He turned to see me. He sure did. But instead of turning his whole body around, instead of pivoting, only his smiling head turned. The rest of him remained turned the other way. I wanted to scream, but I was paralyzed with fear. Realization hit me like a fist to the gut. My mind whirled, and I felt like I was falling, but I didn't move. My god! Nessa had known. She had known I was gonna die soon. That whole conversation we'd had on her porch about what comes after, she was preparing me. Preparing me to face Death. And here he was, dressed up in the skin of my friend Trent.

"He had a hard time letting go of you," said the Trent who wasn't Trent. His voice was still as sweet, though, still as lyrical but without the cadence. "He would have forgotten things sooner if it wasn't for you. There was nothing else to keep him here. No other person who cared for him as much as you did. His last living memory was sent to you, Charlie."

"The b-burning," I answered. I ached to my core remembering the dream. "I let him down. I couldn't be his hero." I was still whirling.

He did not refute this, but he smiled just the same. "Do not mourn for him. He will have greater adventures still." There was a slight echo to his voice, like there were two Trents talking in unison.

"But he won't remember me…"

"No. At least, not yet. But in time."

The woods grew darker and the silver gleam of the trees vanished until all I saw was a small sparkle every so often, trees in sequins. I welcomed the dark. I was relieved that I didn't have to look upon Trent with his nightmarishly twisted form. Behind the Trent who wasn't Trent, there was what I can only describe as a rip in the air and inside it a beautiful golden light, and in that golden light, I saw a sunlit field of barley being brushed by the wind. Around the edges of this portal—because it couldn't be described as a door, being that it was more an expanding tear in my reality—there was a snapping noise like lots of strings giving way, one reality intruding into another.

"What's that?" I asked. "Is that where I'm headed?"

"In time," said the Trent who wasn't Trent. "That's the Evermore. But not now. You have too many memories. Too much pain."

But I wanted to go. I wanted to lay in that field so damn bad it hurt my heart. "Please," I said. "Please take me. Why show up at all when a fella dies if you ain't gonna take him somewhere?"

And somehow Trent was right in front of me, all turned around the right way, with a hand upon my face. "Not now," he whispered, and I closed my eyes because I thought we was gonna kiss. When I opened them again, the Trent who wasn't Trent was gone and it was daylight. I wiped away a tear. I noticed I was still in the woods, but in a deeper area and by a waterfall. Directly beside me, half-covered by brush and bramble, there was a scuffed cello case, and inside of this cello case was a body that no longer had any use.

* * * *

I stayed beside myself for a while, unsure, really, what to do. Death had come for me, but it was just a visit. I wanted to remove all the brush that had been placed to hide the cello case and take a look at who I was one last time, to see my own face. But like in some old ghost movie, my hands were useless on anything made of solid stuff. I was no longer a collection of atoms. I was something completely different. Now I knew even less about myself than I did when I was alive.

I don't know how long I stayed there. I didn't pay no attention to the sun and the moon, to the casting of light among the trees. In time, though—time, by the way, having lost its stout hold over my existence—encouraged by sheer boredom, I began to wander farther and farther from the cello case, gliding over and through the forest with such ease I think I might have smiled. It was a bit like ice skating. And you don't know how freeing it is to have a conversation with a consternated-looking tree, no matter how one-sided, and say, "Mr. Tree, I'm gonna walk through you, and there ain't a damn thing you can do about it," and then proceed to do just as you said you was gonna. In fact, I soon found that death ain't all that bad when a fella realizes he ain't got to worry about finding something to eat or somewhere to shit.

My eyes became sharper in death as well. I began to see things in a new manner, like the way the light literally plays in folds across grass or an echo of sound shimmers like a butterfly through the air. There was so much more to be seen than I ever saw with my human eyes. Most of it was beautiful. Much of it was mysterious. Some of it was dang creepy. Every so often, I thought I saw another soul like me wandering through the woods, but when I'd call to them, they would disappear, like they didn't got the time or the interest.

Once I understood that I wasn't tied to my body by some invisible string and hook, that there weren't no divine laws keeping me where I was, I walked away from the cello case and then out of the woods altogether.

"Stay put," I said to my old self before I left. "I'll be back for you soon. I promise."

I headed for the caretaker's house. I needed to see my only friends in whole world, Leroy and Jimmy. I felt bad for leaving them be for so long.

The night I visited I should have known better than to expect a different vibe from the caretaker's house itself, though. The truth of what existed there gave me the chills. I walked in slowly. The darkness I had always felt in the house was even deeper, more scrubbed into the wood, than I could have ever imagined. I could see a heavy layer of filth on everything, on the walls, on the furniture. It was even gathering on the leftovers in the kitchen. When I was alive, I hadn't been able to see it, but I knew it was there. Seeing it now, though, made me cringe and want to take a bath.

Jimmy was sitting beside Leroy, who was propped up with thin pillows on the bed in the parlor. He was reading to him from the paper. Jimmy looked real tired, and Leroy looked as near a corpse as me. And then I saw the grays. All around Leroy and Jimmy—in fact, all over the house—they began to appear, like they were coming out of hiding. Some were milling about, mindless and hunched over. Some were near the bed, watching my friends with dulled expressions. A few even lifted their dulled eyes and noticed me. I should have been frightened, I know. And truth be told, at first I was. I wanted to run. But then, you can't get deader than dead, I reasoned. What more could they do to me? The grays weren't nothing but people, depressed souls too deep in their mourning to be much of a bother. Their clothes had lost all color, and their faces were milky and drawn. And still, there was a ring of familiarity to them, like I had seen many of these same faces before, but in healthier dispositions. I couldn't imagine where, though. They'd probably been dead for years.

Jimmy was reading the comic pages to Leroy, trying to get him to smile, but all he ever got was a minor annoyed grumble. He would occasionally feel Leroy's forehead, as if the fever would somehow magically break. When he discerned that the fever was still there, he'd give a heavy sigh and then continue reading. There was an ever-present strain, a crack, in Jimmy's voice now. He no longer sounded playful, and it was evident his duty to Leroy was taking its toll. I wanted to help him. I wondered how much sleep he had gotten looking after Leroy all alone. I should have been there for him that last week. For them.

I noticed something unpleasing in the air then, a cold bitterness that cackled like fire burning a favorite memento or letter. I turned to the parlor door and saw, standing there in the dimness of light, a shadow man. He was nothing but the blackest black in the form of a broad-shouldered man wearing a bowler hat. The grays skittered to the edges of the room, some of them disappeared altogether, and the shadow man moved towards the bed. He didn't walk, but he stretched as if the sun were behind him, and then suddenly he was there at the foot of the bed. He stretched again, and now he was laying on top of Leroy like a death shroud and Leroy began to shake and choke under the darkness. Jimmy threw the paper down and tried his best not to freak out. He couldn't see the shadow man, though, so he didn't know what was happening. He just saw Leroy seizing, his face turning a silvery blue.

That fucking thing. That fucking shadow man was hurting my friend. I couldn't just stand by and let it kill Leroy. With all the courage I had left in me, I reached for the shadow. I saw two twisty-turny eyes flash at me like the dream man at the carnival. Still, I grabbed the shadow like a sheet and peeled it off Leroy. I guess it wasn't expecting that, because it shrieked something awful and flew away like a bat. And then, the strangest thing, Leroy saw me.

As he regained his breath he kept looking right at me until he could finally say, "Charlie boy?"

By that time, the shadow man had come back. I saw his eyes again through the mass of darkness, and he was reaching for me, his arms made of black velvety filth. He grabbed me, and I felt a sudden draining of strength, like he was drinking my colors away. I was gonna end up a gray just like those around me. The house grew and stretched, groaned and creaked, like it was all ready to fall apart. I put up a fight, but I was losing. I felt myself falling into a trance-like slumber.

It wasn't until Leroy yelled out in his deep voice, "Get away from him!" that the shadow man's grip lessened enough for me to slide away.

"Get out of here, Charlie!" yelled Leroy as best he could. "Run!"

And I ran, dammit, faster than ever before. Faster than when Bull attacked me and Trent. I could have run all night long, skating across the world. I'm a ghost. Ghosts can run forever.

As I drew near the carnival, I saw the blaze. The castle gate was burning, sending flame, smoke, and ash high into the sky, just one more horror in the night. The dragon who did the deed was still standing in front of it with his dog. He meant it as a warning to me, I suppose. Or maybe he thought I lived in the castle. Maybe he thought he was roasting me the same way he had done Trent. Who knows what a monster thinks?

The dog saw me or felt my presence and started barking, going all kinds of nuts, but seemed too scared to charge me. I had heard before that dogs can sense the dead, and there I was, dead as a doorknob and sending that vicious pup into fits. Good. I strolled near the truck, making sure that dog saw me, and I made the ugliest face I could and howled like a fucking banshee. Well, that scared the bejesus out of the beast. He squealed and jumped into the back of the truck, all tucked into a corner and shaking. Bull was startled by his dog's actions and looked around, maybe to see if the fire department or the police was arriving. When he saw no sign of the law or authority, he got suspicious, cocked his gun as if in warning, fired once at the burning castle gate, and then got into the cab of the truck and quickly drove away. Haunting people is fun. I decided that right then and there. Being haunted isn't. My mind went back to Leroy and the shadow man. I needed to help my friend, but I had no idea how.

I walked through the fire, a metaphor with no one to teach, watching as the wood beams collapsed around me and the sparks danced in the air, and when I came out on the other side, it was two in the morning. The carnival was alive. This time, though, it wasn't empty. I saw people, or spirits, and none of them were gray. They were all as brightly dressed as the fluorescent lights around them. The amusements were going, and there were riders in every one of them. Most of these spirits had deformities on their bodies. They were freaks. There were tall, pale men, bearded women, and men with strange tattoos. There was a man with claws for hands and a boy who walked on his hands because he had no legs. There was a pinhead girl and a lesioned woman so grotesque it was hard for me to look at her. They gave me little more than a nod of acknowledgement, then returned to their carnival. They were used to seeing me even if I ain't ever seen them.

But there was one young man about my age who was standing and watching, his eyes flickering back and forth from me to the burning castle behind me. He was dressed in workers' wear, like he was a carnival hand, and he had a hat like I seen that French skunk wear in those cartoons when I was a kid. You know the ones. His hands were in his pockets, and other than the slight look of surprise on his face, most likely because of my emergence from the burning castle gate, he looked relaxed. I joined him and watched the structure burn.

"Hi," I said. "I'm Charlie."

"Hi," said my new friend. "I was Alfie."

* * * *

Before I left the carnival the next morning, as the sun was rising with the smoke from the castle gate giving everything around a look of foreboding and augury, I asked Alfie how the carnival came to life every night. By that point, most of the other spirits had disappeared into the surrounding woods or were hanging around attractions talking like they's the living. Alfie and me had been talking the night through, and I surmised he was a decent fella.

"We found that with enough of us," came the answer in a lazy shrug of a voice, "if we focus on somethin', we can bring it to life for a bit, especially if it's got some energy in it, some electric power. We can connect with electricity like damn plugs. It's as alive as we was, but as formless as we are."

"But why for only an hour?" I asked him. "And why, for god's sake, at two in the everloving morning?"

He shrugged, kicked at the ground, and said, "We can't do it for too long, and honestly, most of us got other places to haunt. People to get back at or places to see. Two in the mornin' is just the agreed time. Ain't no more reason than that. There's no esoteric purpose, if that's what you was thinkin'."

"Wait. Hold on here. So ghosts have schedules?"

"We're spirits," he said to me with a bit of miff in his voice. "Ghosts are those gray things without color. Echoes of the past without any minds at all. But, yes. Of course we have schedules. Just because we don't know time anymore, don't mean we haven't got the inkling to map out the rest of eternity. I think it's in our nature or something. Keeps us busy. Keeps us thinkin'. None of us wanna go gray."

"Do you have another place to haunt besides the carnival?" I ask him.

He looked sad, and his eyes got all glassy. "No," he said. "The carnival was the only place I ever fit in. I loved it here. I was gonna own this place someday...back when I was Alfie."

From my short time talking with him, I knew that Alfie was a fella prone to exaggeration. I doubted he could ever have really owned the carnival. He told me the strangest tale. He said he had been one of the freaks there at the carnival. That didn't make sense to me, because he was a fine-looking man. Not a blemish on his pretty face. But he winked and said that when he was alive, he had a dick as big and fat as my head, and long too. He said it'd put horses to shame. People'd come from miles around just to have a look at it. For an extra five bucks, he'd offer a few folk personal jack-off shows too. I looked down at his trousers, though, and I didn't see any bulge as big as all that. I think he was just putting me on.

The fire department never showed and eventually the castle gate burned itself out. I walked through the sad ruins and the few remaining cinders and made my way into the woods. I needed to find Nessa. She was the only person I knew who could possibly help me. I had made a promise to my body in the cello case, and I was gonna keep it. So, sure, I needed Nessa to find me. But more importantly, I needed her to protect Leroy from the shadow man. Maybe if she took my body to them she would see the darkness and give them a glamour, whatever that was. Maybe if I'd had her give me a glamour like she said, I'd still be in that body. Coulda woulda but didn't. Nothing for it now, I guess.

I actually saw the glamour as I came upon Nessa's shack. It looked like that fuzziness just above an asphalt road on a hot summer day, but it surrounded the whole shack. It was straight out of a fun-house mirror. Nessa was standing on the porch like she was expecting company. Her face was serious, her brow pinched, and she was looking around, not worried-like, just like she was keeping an eye out. She had that same fun-house effect to her as well. The glamour rippled around her like a fancy aura, playing with colors and light. It wasn't till she started talking that I realized she knew I was there.

"Charlie," she said. "I need you to get on away from here. Ya hear me? Ya can't come into my home. No spirit is allowed to, not for good or ill. Even if the glamour would allow it, I wouldn't. Look down at the ground, child." She was staring right at me now, as if she could see me plain as day. "Spiders is in your wake."

I looked down and sure enough, there were spiders, so many I couldn't count them. They was coming up from the dirt and scampering over from beneath rocks like they was drawn to me. Behind me there was a whole trail, a whole parade of eight-legged critters: hay spiders and black widows and brown recluses, you name it.

"Now get gone," she said. "Go on now."

I spoke, though I knew she couldn't hear me. "I need your help," I said. "Please."

I don't know how messages are relayed between worlds, but she must have understood part of my plea because her face lessened in severity. "I'm sorry, baby," she said. "Ain't nothin' I can do for you now. You're in another realm, another place altogether. My rules don't apply there. But I will find your body. Yes, I will do that for you. But you gotta git now, ya hear? You gotta try to move on, Charlie."

But there was no way for me to move on. I had unfinished business, which I suppose is the very definition of a ghost. Only, according to Alfie, I ain't a ghost at all. I'm a spirit.

* * * *

Nessa kept her word. That very afternoon she came upon me and my body by the falls. I was just visiting, you know, giving myself some company. I don't know how she knew where I was. I think she is more of a witch than she lets on. How else would somebody be able to track a spirit deep into the woods? My spider trail wasn't that long. She had with her a sort of handmade sled tied to a rope.

"I feel ya," she said, pulling the sled to her aft. "I feel ya."

I sat down on a boulder (yeah, I can sit on rock and not worry about sinking into it) and watched as she cleared the cello case of all the bramble and somehow managed to maneuver it onto the sled. That Nessa is a strong woman. She was ever attentive to what she was doing, only occasionally swatting at a fly that was making itself a nuisance. I tell ya, I do not miss flies. The living can keep 'em.

With much more ease than I was expecting, Nessa dragged the cello case up from the falls and through the woods. Her glamour even absorbed my coffin as she held the rope and pulled. She only stopped twice for a rest, and she never spoke to me. But we watched each other. By all the spiders, she could see where I was at all times. I couldn't play hide-and-seek if I wanted to.

It was dusk as Nessa approached the caretaker's house, dragging me in the case behind her on the gravel road. I followed her like I was headed to my own funeral, which I guess I sorta was. Some weak-ass funeral procession, huh?

Me and a bunch of spiders. She stopped at the steps of the house and threw down the rope. She wasn't gonna go in. She just stood there, waiting. I went on ahead of her. The spiders didn't follow me inside, though. I noticed that straight away. There was no shadow man anywhere that I saw, but there were plenty of grays. They were stumbling around the house like guests at a zombie convention.

Leroy was in bed, and the moment I entered his eyes flew wide open, so much so that Jimmy was startled.

"Charlie boy?" Leroy said, looking at me with tears in his eyes. The dim reading lamp cast half of his face in shadow, but I could still see the glistening of tears. "Jimmy, Charlie is here."

"What are you talkin' about, you fool?" said Jimmy, his voice resembling that of the Jimmy I once knew, before he was too tired to play.

"He's right outside," said Leroy in a hush. "Ain't ya, Charlie?"

He gave me a brokenhearted grin. I don't know if he saw, but I gave him one in return. I followed a confounded Jimmy to the front door.

"Hey there, Miss Nessa," Jimmy said, as cordial as a worn-out man can be. His eyes fell on the sled. "What's in the box?"

Nessa couldn't see where I was without the spiders, so to help with matters, I climbed down the steps again and onto the lawn. The spiders danced around my feet in a ballet as I approached myself in the cello case.

"It's your boy," she said. "Somebody done killed your boy."

I heard Leroy's deep sobs coming from inside the house, and I saw Jimmy lose his breath. Just for a moment, I wanted to be alive again. They had loved me. I had been loved in this old world, and now love was tearing them apart.

* * * *

The next day I received something I never thought I would: an honest-to-god funeral. It was only attended by three people—Jimmy, Leroy, and, watching from a distance on the road, Nessa—but it's more than some runaways get. It's more than most get, to be honest. None of my regular customers came, but I suppose I wasn't nothing but a trick to them anyway. And it ain't like my death made the Devlin papers. If it had, if there had been a "Young Male Prostitute Found Dead in Cello Case," the only person who might have shown up to my funeral would have been Patricia, and that would have been more out of decency than any true affection. Patricia don't believe in love.

Jimmy did the digging to lay my body to rest. He'd been at it all morning, going back and forth from me to checking in on Leroy. Finally, Leroy convinced him, after a fair amount of name-calling and consternation, to help him out onto the porch so Jimmy wouldn't need to be going in and out of the house so much, "letting in flies." Nessa helped Jimmy lower me into the earth, and then she backed off again. Not a word was spoken between the two.

Not much was said during the ceremony either, but that's fine. I could see more from Jimmy's eyes than he could ever put into words.

He bit his lip and said, "Look at our boy, Leroy. Just look at him. Ain't he somethin'?"

Leroy was rubbing his eyes as he sat on the swing. "He sure was," he said.

"They loved you, huh?" Alfie was beside me. He'd come along, though I didn't know it until just then. Spirits can go unseen by other spirits just as well as they can hide from people.

"I wish they didn't," I found myself saying. "I hate seeing them so broken up over me. Maybe if they didn't love me, my Death would have taken me. Maybe then I could move on."

"Move on? To what?"

"To what's next. To where we go when we finally forget this life and all its shit. To the Evermore."

His eyes suddenly lit up, and he seemed to grow a little taller. "Oh yeah. I forgot about that."

Some of the other carnival spirits were scattered around the yard and in the trees. It was like Halloween came early. There was the Mermaid Girl and the Octo Man, there was The Man With The Face of Death and the Wolfman, and many more, all of them terribly disturbing and grotesque. How they had all died, I couldn't say. Neither could I tell you what they were doing at my funeral. But there they were. Nessa felt them even if she couldn't see them. I caught her looking over her shoulders more than once.

I was very close to being moved by their attendance. Then I saw where their attention was being drawn. It wasn't to Jimmy as he filled in the dirt atop of the cello case (making me, by the way, the tiniest bit claustrophobic for my old body). The carnival spirits were instead all looking directly at Leroy on the porch. Or rather, they were looking at all the grays who had filed out of the house and were now standing around Leroy on the porch. I noticed there was great grief and anger in my carnival friends' stares. And quite suddenly, as if they'd been caught doing something wrong, the grays shuffled back inside the house walls. No sooner had the last of them vanished than out of the door came a flare of black billowing forth and then seemingly being sucked back in and evaporating again. There was a wild silence. Nothing moved. But slowly my carnival friends began to turn around and make their way back to the trees, some disappearing before they even reached them.

I looked back to the porch, to Leroy, who was smiling at me. With eyes streaming, he waved at me, and so I smiled and waved back.

"You need to stay out of there," Alfie said. "Unless you wanna become a gray yourself. You don't need to be mixin' with their kind."

"That black thing," I said. "Did you see it? What is it? I seen it before in the shape of a man."

"Ain't no man. It's a bit of what was left behind when the caretaker was finally found out." His hands were still in his pockets, his shoulders ready to shrug at the world.

"Found out?"

"He was doin' awful things, Charlie. Such awful things for years and years. Nobody found out until they did. By that point…"

"Well, that black thing, the shadow man, he's hurting my friends."

Alfie looked at me, real sorrow in his eyes. "Ain't nothin' you can do for the livin', Charlie. Best to just let 'em meet their own fates like the rest of us did. Can't do a damn thing."

We'll see about that, I thought to myself.

That night after Alfie had gone on back to the carnival, I sat with my arms wrapped around my knees on the mound of dirt beneath which I lay, and I watched the caretaker's house. Jimmy had planted a sunflower from the back garden on my grave, with a promise to get a proper headstone as soon as he could. He needn't bother, though. A sunflower is much more cheerful than some dreary old stone telling folk of my lack of accomplishments. That flower, the katydids, and the crickets were my only company as I sat there. Well, and those spiders that stayed underfoot like I was their momma, like I would protect them from being squished.

The house lights were on until pretty late. I hoped Jimmy and Leroy were safe, at least for that night, against the shadow man and whatever darkness was in that house. I hoped Jimmy was somehow protecting Leroy. Or maybe Nessa had sensed the harm done and gave them a glamour like was my intent on bringing her here in the first place. They were my family. I knew that now. My family. All I wanted to do was protect them, and I knew I wasn't going anywhere until I saw they were gonna be okay. Evermore can wait. I mean, it'll be there for a while longer yet.

I thought of my family then, the biological one, not the logical one. When I was alive and maybe a little delusional, I went searching for my momma, the one who'd given me up when she was young. I had to do a lot of unsavory things to get that information—who she was, where she was. I couldn't tell you why it was so damn important to me, but it was. A boy's gotta know who his momma is. When I found her, she was a mess, in a hospital with tubes stuck all in her and eyes wandering around like she was lost to all mankind. I don't know what was wrong with her, whether she had given me up because she was sick and knew she couldn't take care of me or if, like so many runaways and hustlers, my momma was an addict and this was her own doing. Either way, she didn't recognize me when I walked into the hospital room. I sat down and stared at her, and she stared back for a good fifteen minutes. We studied each other, but if there was a test given, neither of us would have gotten passing grades. I left the flowers I had brought for her on the foot of the bed, and I never went back to see her after that. I don't know if she's still in that bed or since passed on and is now roaming the halls of that hospital as a gray. Maybe she was able to forget easier than me, though, and she went straight on to the Evermore. It was clear that any memory of me, if she had one, wasn't gonna keep her here. I don't even know who my father was or if I have any brothers and sisters. Don't matter none. They ain't my family anyway.

After a bit, still sitting on my grave, I heard the front screen door squeak and Jimmy came out onto the porch. He stood there for a moment in the dark, looking at my grave. The moon was full and bright. It turned his sad face blue. There were other spirits, maybe elementals, aside from me out that night. I could see them wisping in the air like white clouds of vapor. I wondered if they saw me or even knew of my existence. Maybe, like human people, they're blind to all worlds but their own.

Jimmy stepped from the porch and started walking, slow and languid. I followed him as he made his way through the woods on one of my paths to the carnival. I never thought he knew the way to the carnival. Why would he? But then it hit me that him and Leroy had probably been keeping an eye on me all along. That made me get choked up again. I was "their boy."

Jimmy kicked his way through the ash and debris of the burnt-down castle gate. It was two in the morning. He was a bit thrown by what he saw if the expression on his face was any clue. Ahead of him he saw the lights of the carnival, the Ferris wheel, the carousel, all the rides that still worked a little, glowing like some phantom dream in the night. He walked slowly, hands in his pockets, looking around in wonder as the off-key music played. He even smiled a little. He didn't see the crowd of souls to either side of him watching him with as much curiosity as he was showing the carnival itself. There's the leopard man, there's the ass-faced girl. I walked behind him. Jimmy and me was a two-car parade down the carnival's astral thoroughfare.

He inspected the carnival, the goings-on. I suppose he was there because of me, and that made me want to hug him like I never done in life. He opened the gate to the haunted house and stood there for a moment, wondering, I guess, if he had the nerves to go on in. The entire population of the carnival seemed to be trailing us, their faces and half-faces indecipherable. Even Alfie's face was more stone than spirit. They didn't follow us into the haunted house when Jimmy finally crossed its threshold, though. I nearly didn't go inside either.

At first, everything inside looked the same as it had when I was alive and had dared to come in. There was the same rotting furniture, dusty mirrors, and ghoulish mannequins in grotesque poses. Unsettling, but nothing new. But then a horrifying realization hit me as I investigated one of the mannequins more thoroughly with Jimmy: this was no mannequin at all. This was The Man With The Face of Death. This had, at one time, been an actual person who had been stuffed like some hunted animal after he had died. My god, and there was the Mermaid Girl in a large busted tank. I looked around and suddenly understood why the faces of those at the carnival and even some of the grays at the caretaker's house looked so damn familiar.

Perhaps my feelings of unease about the place were transferring to Jimmy. Or perhaps he just didn't want anything more to do with the haunted house past the front parlor. Either way, we were soon back outside, and I was thankful for it. The carnival folk were still there waiting for us, an audience of the long dead. I understood then why they looked at Jimmy so strangely. Here was a man, an actual flesh and blood man, and he was going to see what had become of some of them. Only he would never guess the mannequins weren't anything more than factory-made props. Would he? I wondered if some of them had higher hopes.

Jimmy came to the log ride and stopped. I had never told him I lived there, but it was the most logical place, being that the haunted house was too creepy, even for a skeptic like Jimmy. I had figured out by now that this was why he was at the carnival, to find some piece of me still here, a remembrance to smile at while holding. He followed the rickety tracks to the very top of the stalled ride. There he discovered my log, made comfortable with blankets, a few items of clothing, and a half-eaten bag of chips. He crouched down, picked up one of my stained tank tops, held it to his face, and started to cry. I sat with him for a while until he felt well enough to make the journey outside. He carried my tank top with him. It's strange, the things we choose to remember other people with.

The carnival was dead once more as we made our way down the thoroughfare. He didn't seem to notice this, though. Only the dead and the dying were on his mind, which is strange when you think about it. Here he was, thinking about me, a dead guy, bringing me into his mind with descriptive force, when all around him that night the carnival folk were disappearing, just vanishing into the air. Some going back to wherever they roamed at other hours. And some…some just seemed to wane with a smile—like the Mermaid Girl and The Man With The Face Of Death. For some reason, I got the distinct feeling I'd never see those two again.

* * * *

Before Jimmy set foot back into the house, I knew there was something not right. The only way I can explain it is like I seen these waves, folds in the air, coming from the caretaker's house as we approached. The grays were moaning. They weren't exactly distressed, but they were confused and their confusion manifested itself in a way that made me want to pull Jimmy back. Whatever was in the house at that moment, it was not the shadow man. The grays seemed to have an acceptance of that particular demon. No, this was something else.

Jimmy paused at the screen door when he saw it was wide open. I saw the hairs on the back of his neck stand on end and his breathing became shaky and halting. I went in ahead of him and noticed the grays standing in a great milky mass at the parlor entrance. They did not seem to notice my arrival. Instead, they all seemed quite interested in a corner to the side of the front parlor, just behind the door. Something was crouched there, hidden by the dark. I recognized the form too late. Just as Jimmy crossed the threshold into the caretaker's house, Bull emerged from the shadow, his face glowing with a deviant light, and he hit Jimmy over the head with the butt of his shotgun, producing a horrifying crack.

Jimmy hit the floor hard enough to knock the life out of him. Bull was on him at once as Jimmy curled up, defending himself from each blow and kick that hillbilly gave him. Jimmy was conscious, but he was pulling away, crawling in the wrong direction. All the heavy furniture or possible weapons for defense were in the parlor where Leroy lay or in the kitchen. Jimmy was going for the stairs. He was gasping and grunting in agony with every knock from that bully. And I was helpless. I couldn't do a damn thing but watch as my friend, my family, got beat to death by a raged-out human monster. I began to cry out to the grays, asking them to wake up, to help, but they just stared at me like I was speaking a foreign language.

"You fucking assholes!" I screamed. "Do something! Help him. Or at least tell me what to do!"

But that was my mistake. Leroy heard me somehow and woke up in his bed in the parlor.

"Charlie boy!" he yelled.

I realized then why Jimmy was pulling the wrong way. He was trying to get Bull away from Leroy, and here I'd done brought the asshole's full attention right to him. Bull looked at Leroy with a hungry grimace, then gave Jimmy one last kick to the ribs. Jimmy tried to cry out as Bull headed for Leroy, but he was in too much pain. All he could do was sob.

I was furious. Absolutely furious with myself, with the grays, with Bull, with the whole damn situation. My anger reached back and dragged everyone who'd ever wronged me to mind—Carter, Patricia, even my momma. I had never been more angry or frightened. Bull stood over Leroy, grabbing a pillow from beneath my friend's head. This was no good. This was no fucking good t'all. Not thinking, I reached for a small glass that was half-full of water sitting on the nightstand near me, and I threw it at Bull. It took a moment for it to register that I had indeed thrown it. Somehow, wrapped up in all my rage, I'd picked up that glass of water and hurled it at Bull's head. Worlds had interacted. It knocked him back and he fell to the floor. The glass spilt everywhere but didn't break, rolling away from him instead. Well, it didn't take me long to realize how useful passion can be in the afterlife. In fact, I imagine that lesson was learned in about two seconds. I started picking up and tossing everything I could get my non-hands on.

Bull was terrified. I even managed to draw some blood from the bastard when I cracked a plate over his head. He didn't know where to look as I threw the unbroken glass again from one side of him and then raced to the other and tossed a small wood stool.

Soon he was screaming, and he ran from the house like he'd been threatened by the devil himself. I watched him go from the porch with a smile on my face. Walking back inside the house, the grays were now all focused on me, but I didn't have time to care. I raced to Jimmy's side. His breath had become ragged, and he was shaking. His eyes were closed, and he looked clammy and white beneath all the blood.

"Find Nessa!" I heard Leroy's deep voice from the bed. "Charlie, if you're here, go find Nessa. Now. Please!"

I hated leaving both of them there in such bad shape, especially with the shadow man and now Bull wanting them dead, but what else could I do? I sprinted from the house and into the woods, and the passion with which I ran created a small breeze. Yards flew by in seconds. I ran, yelling and screaming the whole way, hoping that, like the grays, my agitation might wake Nessa the hell up. I knew she had a connection to the afterlife so I didn't see a flaw in this thinking. And turns out, I was right. I met her as she was coming out of her shack. Dammit, I would have drilled through that glamour somehow if she hadn't met me.

"You've got a way about you," she said as she walked with a burlap sack over one shoulder. "You could wake the dead or stone the livin' with the ruckus you just made." I was impatient, trying to get her to walk faster. "I'm hurryin'," she said. "I still got legs. Cain't fly through these woods like you, Charlie."

Nessa was hesitant to go into the caretaker's house when we arrived, but then she breathed deep and said, "There's foulness in here that shouldn't be smelt by no one."

Inside, we found Leroy, who'd crawled from his bed, cradling Jimmy on the floor. "He's still alive," Leroy said, "just barely. Can you help him, Miss Nessa?"

She looked him over. "Oh, baby. I can take him to the clinic, that's about it. He done had some real damage done to him."

"It's Bull," I said, my rage returning. "It's Bull that done it."

"Hush, Charlie," she said. "I know who done it."

Leroy looked shaken by this. "You feel him too?" he asked. "You feel Charlie?"

"NASA could feel Charlie, most likely," she said. "That boy got a stronger will than most spirits I ever came across." She grabbed Jimmy under his arms, trying to hoist him up. "I'm gonna need to drag him to the car, Leroy. Don't mean no disrespect by it."

Jimmy was still breathing ragged when Nessa peeled out of the drive in the Buick. I went back inside and watched over Leroy, whom Nessa had helped back into his bed.

"You still here, Charlie?" he asked. He was beat in every way a man could be beat. "I want to say thank you. Thank you for losin' your temper and scarin' away Bull. You might have just saved Jimmy's life. We was talkin' this afternoon about findin' a new place to live. Not because of you. Or rather, it is a bit. To be truthful, without you this place feels different. If we had any balls"—he started drifting—"we'd have forced you to come and live here, no arguments. But then…the grays…and the shadow…"

I wanted to say to him *Yes! Yes! Leave here.* But he was asleep. He could not have heard me.

That dark, filthy feeling came over the place again. I noticed the grays were fading into the walls, backing into them, not wanting to stay but afraid to avert their gazes. They vanished fast enough, though, once the shadow man made himself known. I saw the quickness of shadow escape around the parlor door like a cape. Maybe still juiced from the night's ordeal, still angry, I left Leroy's side and decided to investigate. Halfway up the stairs to the second floor, I saw the shadow man. He was just sorta standing there in the dark, watching me, and I watched him right back. He froze my anger solid, iced it into fear. Then, in a blink, he slid up the stairs, and his darkness mixed with the night until I couldn't see any difference between the two.

* * * *

I stayed with Leroy that night at the house. I didn't know what use I could be against the shadow man if he chose to come back, or, for that matter, Bull, but I was gonna do my best. Leroy didn't wake the entire night, though. There were no more visits from monsters, living or dead, and the grays didn't bother us neither. In fact, Leroy slept through the next day, mumbling every now and then for Jimmy, but with no real commotion other than that.

It was midafternoon when I spotted a fancy silver car coming down the drive towards the caretaker's house in a storm of dust, followed by a big ambulance. At first, I thought it was Jimmy being brought back to the house, but Nessa had driven him to the clinic in that old Buick of Leroy's, not this showboat. When a man and a woman got out of the car with similar features to Leroy, I knew what had happened. The doc at the clinic, concerned that Leroy was sick and alone, had somehow gotten hold of his family and told them where he was. This had to be Leroy's brother and sister.

The brother, a stout thing who was overdressed in a suit and tie and paying for it dearly with streams of perspiration, put his hands on his hips and looked at the house.

"This is where our Leroy's been livin'?" he said, clearly disgusted. Whereas Leroy's voice was a deep, heavy thing, this man's was too light and airy for his looks.

"A home's a home, I guess," said the woman. She was as tall as Leroy. Wearing a blue summer dress, she was fanning herself with a glossy magazine.

"But, Gladys, look at it." Her brother looked about to have a conniption. "I mean, just look at it. I bet this was all that Jimmy's doin'. Leroy would never have chosen to live in a place like this. He was raised with tastes, with standards."

"Ernie, you think Leroy would live anywhere he didn't want to? This was his choice of home as much as it was Jimmy's. Now, let's go find him." She motioned to the EMTs to follow. "That doctor said our poor brother wasn't doin' well at all. I'm a bit scared what we're gonna find in there."

"We'll get him home with family where he belongs," said Ernie. He leaned on the railing as he mounted the steps. "Then we'll take him to a real doctor and get him fixed up."

"What about Jimmy? What do we do about him?"

"I think it's best—and Mama and Daddy agree with me," he said, facing her on the porch, "that Leroy just forgets about Jimmy. And that's the end of that."

They were clearly appalled by the living situation when they entered the house, walking in as if they were expecting the floorboards to give out beneath their feet any minute.

"This is filthy," Ernie said. "Hasn't been cleaned in weeks. Look at all these broken dishes lying about. You'd think they'd be able to hire a maid service, what with all that money Leroy inherited from Uncle Howard. What have they been usin' it for?"

Gladys saw Leroy unconscious in the bed and, gasping, hurried over to him. "Sweet Jesus!" she exclaimed. "He looks much worse than that doctor let on. Why, look at him, Ernie. He's at death's door."

"Leroy!" shouted Ernie into his brother's ear. "Leroy! My, my, my. Now do you think we should tell Jimmy we're taking our brother home, dear sister? Because I think we should charge him with attempted murder."

The EMTs rushed over and checked Leroy's vitals before hoisting him onto a gurney. The grays were all around now, drab spectators. Maybe they were expecting me to do something. I don't know. All I was thinking was that maybe Ernie was right. Perhaps it would be best to get Leroy out of the caretaker's house and away from Bull and the shadow man. Then when Jimmy got better, he could go find Leroy, and they could move somewhere new, just like Leroy said they was talking about doing.

"Still," said Gladys, "Jimmy deserves to know what's happened. It wouldn't be kind to leave him an empty house with no word of where we've taken Leroy."

"What's happened, dear sister, is Leroy left him. That's all he needs to believe. We ain't gonna say another word to him." They followed the gurney back outside with Leroy still oblivious as to what was happening. Ernie looked back at the house, dabbing his tie to his forehead sweat. "And good riddance to this place and to Jimmy."

I had had enough of that prick disparaging my friend like that, and I'm afraid I let my temper get the better of me.

I kicked the dirt and sent a couple spiders flying through the air. They landed on Ernie's wrist and he flicked them off with a shudder.

"And flyin' spiders too," he said. "Don't that beat all."

They got in their snazzy car and drove off, ambulance leading the way, just as Nessa came barreling back down the drive in the old blue Buick. She pulled over and let them pass, then got out of the car and watched Leroy's family disappear behind a cloud of dust. She looked towards the house, towards me. She kept her eyes to the ground as I approached, the spiders ever my giveaway.

"We're gonna need to watch after Jimmy when he gets home," Nessa said. "I knew they was comin' to get Leroy. But I didn't think it'd be so soon. He gonna need protection in that house all alone. He gonna be a changed man without Leroy. Understand me, Charlie?"

I thought I did.

"You're gonna have to get in his head, in his dreams."

I was wrong. I had no idea what she was talking about.

"Learn to do that, Charlie," she said. "It's the only hope he got. It's the only way we're gonna make Bull pay for what he done. To both of us."

I wondered what she meant by 'both of us.' But, of course, Nessa didn't explain any further, as was her way. Her cryptic demeanor was getting on my damn nerves. I mean, my god! I was a damn ghost, and I wasn't half as cryptic as she.

So I walked into Devlin. I stayed to the shoulder of the road the whole way. There was no real reason to do this. I could walk straight down the middle of the highway and let the cars and trucks pass right through me without so much as a hair out of place, but I thought that might get annoying after a bit, hearing snippets of stories I would never know the beginnings or ends to from families and groups of strangers. I never liked cliffhangers, especially when there wasn't a hill in the first place.

I wasn't the only spirit or ghost on the highway. There were quite a few, in fact. Some of them I could see as clear as day. Others shielded themselves from my sight, preferring to be alone. I still felt them around me, though. There were a few still locked in the grief and disbelief of their passing: teenagers sitting in a circle around the spot where they had died five years before, most likely in a car wreck; an old woman in clothing from decades ago crying and wailing under a light pole for someone to help her; a young man in a hardhat and a uniform still hanging upside down from the telephone wire where he had been electrocuted. Who knows if any of them will ever move on? Who knows if I will? There was a sobering thought.

Devlin itself was pretty much the same, except now I saw the invisible inhabitants. Ghosts wandered around a lot but never get very far. And I understood then what the difference was between a ghost and a spirit. They both want answers, but only a spirit will go looking for them.

Thankfully, there weren't a lot of ghosts in the clinic. At first, I figured there hadn't been a lot of death there. It was a clinic, after all, not a hospital. When people die, they die in hospitals. But then I realized even the dumbest ghost wouldn't want to stay in a hospital or a clinic. They'd try to find some place comfortable to mope around in, some place more familiar. The only spirit I crossed paths with in the clinic was an older doctor. He smiled and nodded like he'd seen me there before, which, of course, he had when I came to visit Leroy. This was that doctor's home. This was where he had felt the most comfortable in life.

I found Jimmy easily enough in the very same room Leroy had been in. He was cleaned up, but was still bruised and unconscious, with all sorts of wires and machines attached to him. I decided I'd sit with him. What else did I have to do?

It was two days later when he finally woke up. I was there beside him when it happened, and strangely enough, I think I was in his head. Just for the briefest of moments, I believe I was doing what Nessa told me I should. It happened just so: As he was waking up, I seen him, but he wasn't lying on the bed. I mean, his body was still there, but he wasn't. No, he was sitting directly across from me, free of bruises, staring at himself and then looking at me. His eyes grew wide and then BAM. He was awake again, disoriented and mumbling.

Nessa came in soon after. I don't know if she'd been contacted somehow or if she had just sensed he was awake, but there she was, holding his hand like an old friend. That was strange in and of itself. Before Nessa brought my body to the caretaker's house, I'd never seen so much as a nod between the two.

"Where's Leroy?" Jimmy asked when he had cleared his head. "Did Bull…?"

She hushed him. "Bull didn't do nothin' to Leroy," she answered. "He just fine. You just need to get yourself better."

But Jimmy ain't a dummy. He could tell by her voice something was different. "What ain't you tellin' me, Miss Nessa?" he asked all suspicious-like.

"He gone, Jimmy," she said without pause. "His family came and got him, seein' that you couldn't take care of him. They took him home. To their home, I suspect."

"And he went with them…willingly?" Jimmy asked. "He didn't put up a fight? Nothin' at all?"

"I wasn't there," she said. "I can't say."

Sometimes you can see a heart break as clear as cracked ice. Jimmy's face could not hide it. "He left me," he whispered.

I wanted to tell him that it wasn't so. I wanted to assure him that Leroy had been unconscious when they took him. I screamed this in Nessa's ear, but all she could sense was my irritation.

"He left me," Jimmy said again as his lips started to tremble.

"You don't know that," Nessa said. "Hush, baby. Wait for the story to unfold."

"Yes, I do," cried Jimmy. "I do know it. He wouldn't let them take him if... But he did. He left me!"

And then he began to howl like a wounded dog. His cries filled the clinic. Nessa did nothing to quiet him. Guess she thought it was best he get it out of his system. I couldn't help myself. I joined him. We howled together. We, the wounded and forgotten.

* * * *

Jimmy went home to the caretaker's house two days later. Nessa drove the Buick, and he lay down in the backseat. He never said a word, just laid there the whole ride home in the fetal position under a thin clinic blanket. You might have thought he was still in a coma if his eyes weren't open, staring at nothing with a dullness like wet paint. I sat in the front with Nessa but kept watch on him.

Every now and then, Nessa would say something to Jimmy like "You doin' okay back there?" or "Do you wanna stop for anythin'?" but she never got an answer. Finally, she told him, "You need to leave that house, Jimmy. That house ain't no good for ya. Weren't no good for Leroy either. It's a good thing he left. Believe me. If he hadn't left it, he'd most likely be dead by now. That house has darkness in it, a deep shadow that's been festerin' there for years." She kept her eyes on the road and her hands on the wheel as she spoke. "Think about it, Jimmy," she said. "Think about leavin' that place. I know you hear me."

I think she knew he wasn't listening to her. He was off somewhere in his own head, draped in misery. But perhaps somehow her words would get through.

In a lowered voice, she said to me, "Charlie, you need to get him out of there. You've got more spunk than any ghost I ever knew. I said so to Leroy, remember? You're a ghost with a stubborn spirit. Convince him to get out of there. That place will only drag him deeper into the black if he stays."

Nessa helped him into the house, but then left quickly, disappearing into the woods with a couple of hesitant backwards glances. I don't know what she expected me to do. The lines of communication between me and Jimmy weren't exactly flowing.

Jimmy took a standing look around the house, like maybe Leroy was there after all, and then, being disappointed, crawled into the bed in the parlor. The grays came out of the walls, but they wasn't interested in Jimmy. Some of them were looking at me now, and their expressions weren't blank but curious. I made my way past them and looked out the back door to the garden. It was more overgrown now than ever, many of the vegetables going to waste, the chickens loose and feeding on the others. Fall was coming soon. If Jimmy didn't harvest what he'd grown soon, he was gonna lose everything. I doubt he'd starve, though. Leroy was smart about storing food for the colder months. The pantry was well stocked for a year at least.

I felt the chill of fear in the air. I knew the shadow man was behind me. He was watching me. Maybe he was even thinking about trying to rape me again. That's what it had felt like when he attacked me before: a violation. A rape. I turned in time to see him disappear quickly down the hall, like a black cape in the wind. Then I heard his darkness creeping up the stairs…and I followed him. I followed the shadow man. Why? Maybe I was just getting tired of being afraid of him. Maybe I was doing it for Jimmy. Either way, I decided to face the faceless.

I was led to the attic, a place I had never been and, by the looks of it, neither had Jimmy or Leroy. It was a dark, dusty place, nothing special at first glance, just wood beams at angles and not one piece of furniture. But it was clear this room had been used at one time. There were deep scuffs on the floor, hooks on the walls and the ceiling, and an old rusty sink by a triangular window that looked out over the front yard. I could see my grave from up here. The shadow man was nowhere. The room creaked with his presence, though. Any other sound seemed to crawl away with the fading sunlight on the floorboards. I stayed near the attic door for the most part. That place made me uneasy.

Then as my eyes locked onto a blackness in a far corner, the attic seemed to stretch. The wood even whined. A great fear came over me. The blackness grew until it was the shadow man, and he stood ten feet high, at least. I felt like I had been tossed into a dream. The shadow man grew a face, the twisty-twirly face I knew from the carnival nightmare. He reached for me, but I swung away.

"Get out of here!" I yelled over a groan that had come from nowhere but was now everywhere. "You leave my friend Jimmy alone." And then as if I knew something that the darkness didn't, I said, "Or I'll make you pay."

The shadow man let out a terrifying holler. He reached deep inside his darkness and pulled from it something red and glowing. With a flick, it rolled off a wisp of gloom and fell to my feet, where it broke like a Faberge Egg. A red mist rose around me with terrible speed, showing me a scene of carnage from this very room, a scene of a young girl being butchered alive by a gleeful physician. I swatted at the mist until it vanished, but the girl's screams remained. They pushed me down the first few steps, and I ran the rest of the way. Jimmy wasn't aware that I had climbed into bed with him like a terrified child. I don't know if he felt my arms around him, holding tight, wishing the bloody images away. I don't even know if I was much comforted myself. But at least I wasn't alone.

I laid there with Jimmy, still hearing that poor girl's screams, my arms wrapped around my friend but not really touching him at all, for a good portion of the night. In time, I stopped shaking. The shadow man made no appearance, but the grays were all around us. They had taken a keener interest in me, some more than others. One of them, a tall man with a pointy head, sat on the foot of the bed, his face pale in the light. I honestly didn't know the grays could do anything but fumble about and pass through walls, but here this one was, choosing to have a seat. He was staring right at me with a slight glimmer of lucidity in his eyes, like a tiny blade of grass peeking through fallen snow. I sat up slowly.

"What's your name?" I asked. I kept a scowl on my face just in case he was an unfriendly.

He heard the question. I saw it register. But he said nothing. He did, however, move his mouth, like he was copying the movement of mine or just discovering the use of his.

"Why can't you speak?" I continued. "Is it because of the shadow man? Are you afraid of him? He did something to you, didn't he?"

No words. I stood to see if his eyes would follow me. They did. There was consciousness there. This fella was waking.

"What's your name?" I repeated. "What did the shadow man do to you?"

Some of the other grays were interested in what was going on now and began to shuffle nearer to the bed.

"If I told you that I was gonna find a way to rid this place of the shadow man, would you help me?"

The man's mouth dropped open and hung that way.

"Ain't nothing in the world, living or spirit, that can't be gotten somehow, understand me? The world's too much a pretty place to have something so ugly calling the shots. I'm gonna find out how to git the shadow man and git him good. But I might need your help. Can you help me?"

Still not a thing. But he was listening. His eyes were coming back, goddammit.

"I need you to stay here and look after Jimmy, just for a bit. Can you do that? I'm heading to the carnival. I have a few questions to ask a friend of mine who lives there. You just stay here on the bed and watch Jimmy. Don't let the shadow man come near, okay?"

I doubted the grays could do a damn thing against the shadow man, especially since it was the shadow man who made them grays in the first place by my reckoning. But that glimmer of interest in the gray man's eyes gave me hope. He still had some fight left. And I needed to get to

Alfie at the carnival. I thought it better to leave Jimmy with a weak defense than no defense at all.

"I'll be back," I said. "I'll be quick."

The gray man with the pointy head stayed seated on Jimmy's bed as I left.

* * * *

I called for Alfie once I was at the carnival. I didn't feel like going looking for him. He made himself seen, walking towards me as he was appearing—half a face, a shoulder, an arm—one piece of the puzzle at a time and in motion until he stood face in front of me. I told him all that had happened, how Jimmy got beaten and taken off to the clinic, how Leroy's family came and got him and now Jimmy thinks Leroy left him, and I told him all about my confrontation with the shadow man.

"How come you're not a gray?" he asked me, his face showing more emotion than I had ever seen it do. The boy was shocked. "How did he not suck the color right out of ya? I've seen him do it."

I shrugged. "I dunno," I said. "I pulled away, was all. I needed to go downstairs, to protect Jimmy. That's all that was on my mind. But I sure could use your help with something back there."

He studied me over for a moment, then, without a word, started walking. "Well," he said, turning to look at me when he saw I was still standing where I'd been. "You comin' or ain't ya?"

Alfie didn't like the grays one bit. It was like he didn't even want to touch them. He leered at them as if his leers and animosity even registered with them. To my surprise, the gray man with the pointy head was still on the bed with Jimmy. He rose when he saw us and then joined the others of his kind, though he didn't mill about anymore. He just stood there in the midst of his stumbling gray brothers and sisters and watched us.

"That was Cal," said Alfie, shaking his head all condescending-like. "He was one of the animal tamers, one of the normals." Alfie glanced at the other grays. "Looking around here, all of these grays are normals. I don't see a freak in the whole lot. None of my own kind at all."

Jimmy was still asleep, or at least, his eyes were closed. He was unshaven and pale.

"What do ya need from me?" asked Alfie, still giving the stink eye to any gray who looked his way.

"I need to get into Jimmy's head," I said. "Rather, I need you to show me how to get into his head."

"Like in his dreams?" Alfie seemed incredulous. "Boy, I don't know how to do that shit. I live in the goddamn carnival. I hardly see any of the livin' at all. How would I know what goes on in their heads?"

Well, that was plain discouraging, let me tell you.

"Your friend looks too ill to live, though," he said, nodding at Jimmy.

"Don't you say that!" I exclaimed. "He's gonna live. He's got to. He's gotta find Leroy. I don't want any of that negativity around here."

He snorted out a laugh. "Boy, this house ain't got no energy but the negative kind."

I gave him the stink eye for that.

"Alright, alright," he said, holding up his hands in a show of retreat. "But it sounds to me you're lookin' for a happy endin' where none may exist, Charlie. I don't know what good getting' in his head would do, anyway. Who knows if you'd be able to find him once you got in there."

He was right, of course. I didn't know a thing about the maps of the mind, the hidden corridors of the soul. Jimmy could be so deep inside himself I'd like to never find him or find my way out even if I did.

Alfie's attention was drawn to that painting on the wall that I had brought over from the haunted house, the one of the pretty girl. He stood so close to it I thought he might vanish into the wall.

"Did you know her?" I asked.

"Sure," he said. "All us freaks knew her. She was the prettiest normal at the carnival. A real rose. She was my gal…for a bit. Her name was Flora." A hint of a smile shown on his face, but it was a sad smile and was soon gone like blown dust. "But she didn't love me. Not really. I was just a plaything for her, but she gave me up as soon as the caretaker came lookin' for a new toy."

He continued to stare at the painting for a while. I thought it inappropriate for me to pull him away, so I stood beside him, let him alone to his pain and rage. But then something new happened in this fun house that wasn't no damn fun. The painting began to change. At least, that's what it seemed to me. The face began to stretch forward and the colors all bled away. Alfie saw it too and gasped a "Holy shit!"

I realized what was happening. Flora the gray was passing through the wall where Flora the painting hung. Just a creepy coincidence. Alfie was having none of it, though. There he stood, face to face with this girl whose beauty had long since left her, and all he could say was a tearful, "Goddamn fuckin' bitch."

He raced past me and from the house. When I got to the door, he had already vanished into the woods. Flora wasn't bothered. She stood where we had left her, staring into nothingness. But Cal…he was right at my shoulder, staring out the door alongside me.

That night, I walked right into Jimmy's head, just like it was part of the house. I kid you not. I had been thinking about how to get in there all day with no answers. There had to be a way. Alfie had proven useless, the poor fella, and I'd given up asking the grays anything. Every so often, I'd see Cal watching me, but I still wasn't able to get word one from him. It was his stares that got me up and walking around the house. I did not like the feeling his eyes were giving me, of being examined, studied. So as I was wandering through the house, pondering harder than I ever did in life, I decided to take a look at the basement. I had never been in there, but as far as I knew, that was where Leroy put his canned vegetables from Jimmy's garden.

I started walking down the stairs into the dark, one lazy step at a time, and then, quite inexplicably, things leveled off way too soon. I hadn't gone down four steps before I felt flat surface again. That was a sorry-ass basement if that was its total depth. Ahead of me, I saw naught but a long hall with great arched doorways leading to rooms on either side. A red glow lit the place. Looking back, I no longer saw the door to the basement, only more hallway. *What the hell?* I thought, so I kept walking. The rooms—and there were many of them—were empty, but the air was filled with whispers, worried voices falling over each other like a waterfall, like mixed conversations or a party where everyone is freaking out and no one is listening to the host. The host has done left.

I called, "Hello?" but I was ignored. I recognized Jimmy's voice through the jumble, and I picked up speed, looking in every room and calling for him rather excitedly. I needed to find him and fast. I didn't know how long I was gonna be able to stay in his head, if there were rules about such things, or, indeed, if I was ever gonna be able to get out again. But I needed to find Jimmy, both for his and Leroy's sake.

I followed the dark hallway until it let out into a spiral staircase bigger than any I'd ever seen or imagined. Everything looked to be made of dark bone, banisters and steps both. Down down down, the stairs went into a red abyss and, over my head, up up up too. But I wasn't headed up. I needed to get to the bottom of things, so I started walking. Still, on my descent, there were more empty rooms to the side, all of them at odd angles. Somehow, I knew Jimmy wouldn't be in any of them, though. I was positive I was gonna find him below. That's where the whispers, cries, and sobs were coming from.

I started sprinting down the steps, faster and faster, until the whispers weren't whispers but overlapping voices crashing into one another with some violence. It was all so confusing, I wasn't sure at one point whether the voices were coming from right in front of me or if I had done passed Jimmy by. Then I saw him. The staircase poured out onto a large white floor that was blushed with red. Everywhere there were empty bowls and broken coffee cups, seemingly clean or never used. Sitting on the end of a grand ol' bed, one of those like Patricia had with a large dark headboard, was Jimmy. At least, it was a version of Jimmy. He looked old, much older than he was, with a long white beard and eyes puffy from tears.

"Charlie?" he said, taking note of me. He looked to be having trouble just keeping his head up and staying focused. The voices around us quieted down. "Charlie boy, is that you? You look so thin. You should eat. I'd offer you somethin', but without Leroy..." He gestured to all the scattered dishes.

I caught sight of my arms. He was right. I did look thin. I was a skeleton, a damn Halloween costume.

"Why did he leave me, Charlie?" Jimmy asked sleepily. "Was I so bad to him? Was I so ornery?"

"No," I assured him, coming closer to the bed. "Leroy didn't leave you at all, Jimmy. He did nothing of the sort."

"He's not here. If he didn't leave me, where did the asshole go?" The voices around us rose in irritation.

"He was taken from you," I said. "He was taken by his family. Nessa told you this. They done took him back to where they live. You gotta go find him, Jimmy. Then everything will be okay."

I sat beside him on the bed. He looked at me, eye to eye.

"If he went with them," he said, "well, then, once he realized what they had done, he would have fought to come back home, come back to me. Everything will most certainly not be okay, Charlie. No, no, no. Everything is broken now."

A large crack, like bone breaking, permeated the hall.

"Jimmy, Leroy was real sick. You saw how ill he was. He couldn't fight back even if he had woken up. He ain't got the strength."

"Why hasn't he come to me here, in my dreams? I haven't seen him in my dreams, not once. I miss his face so much. Why did he leave me?" His voices were wailing again. They were nearly deafening.

"Jimmy, ain't you listening? He didn't leave you. Maybe he's in a coma. Maybe he can't come to you right now, neither in dreams nor in life, because he's not got the ability."

Jimmy gave a weak grin and took my boney hands in his. "I've missed you, Charlie boy," he said. "I'm sorry. I'm real sorry about the way I treated you before you died. If I had known…"

"You didn't do nothing wrong. No need to apologize, Jimmy."

"Oh, yes… Yes, there is. I was dismissive. I wanted Leroy all to myself. I wanted to be the only one takin' care of him, the only one who could bring a smile to his face." He cradled my skull in his wrinkled palms. "But you were our boy. And now you're gone…and Leroy's gone. And I'm alone."

Alone…alone…so alone… repeated the whispers as they trailed off into bone-red nothingness.

"Go find him," I said. "Goddammit! You don't have to be alone, Jimmy. Go find Leroy."

And in an instant, blackness suffocated the bone hall. At first, I thought it was a symptom of Jimmy's depression, but then there was a breeze like death that tumbled down the stairs, filling the chamber like a pond. The breeze became a wind, and the wind became a storm, and the storm became a cyclone. Dishes were picked up and went flying in the cyclone, round and round, until they were sucked upward with terrible force. The winds got stronger still, and Jimmy and me clung to the bed, his voices asking the question that was also going through my mind.

What is this?

But that sense of rape, of violation and stripping of color, told me exactly what was happening. I had let my guard down and now the shadow man had us both. I hollered at Jimmy to hold tight to the bed, and he hooked an arm around a bedpost. But it was too late for me. I was soon swept up into the hurricane of blackness, being tossed along with the broken dishes and scraps of staircase.

Just when I was about to give up, thinking I'd let the shadow man have me because what else could I do, a light broke through. The dishes and bone stopped in midair and fell. I could see Jimmy still sitting on the bed, but I was pulled up and out, into the brightness. I found myself back in the caretaker's house, being flung across the floor of the parlor and landing near the bay window. Nessa was on the bed, standing over Jimmy, straddling him, but not facing him. She was facing the shadow man who hung in the air like an angry cloud. I was catching the end of a confrontation. With a shake of her fist and a few sharp words I didn't understand, Nessa chased the shadow man away. He fled with a roar up the stairs, and Nessa, breathing heavy, collapsed onto Jimmy's legs. It was only then I saw what she had done. She'd given Jimmy a glamour. Jimmy was still in his self-induced coma, though. He didn't seem to notice a thing.

Nessa got off the bed and spoke to the air. "Charlie," she said, "you be okay to get in his head now. But just you. Nobody else. I fixed the glamour so it's so. It's a good thing you're making friends on the other side, or I wouldn't have known to come save your ass. My word, you get yourself in trouble more than my brother Ray did."

Friends? I wondered. And then I felt a slight touch on my arm, somebody helping me up. It was Cal. Cal had left the house. He had somehow told Nessa I was in trouble.

"Thank you," I said.

He stared at me blankly, then walked back into the wall.

I followed Nessa as she walked into the kitchen and past the host of curious grays. The fact that even one of their number had grown curious was startling. A whole gaggle of them showing interest…well, that was mind-boggling. Nessa stood with a hand on the back door. She turned and looked in my direction, though not, of course, directly at me.

"Well, come on, then," she said. "You and me need to talk face to face." And then she stepped into the back garden, startling the chickens. When I stepped outside, I did not find myself in Jimmy's overgrown garden at all, though. I was in some place completely new to me. Nessa was allowing me inside her own head. That was a place far more striking than the bone hallways and stairs of Jimmy's mind.

I walked, awestruck, through a grand palace of marble columns and plush lounge chairs, past potted plants that reached taller than me and murals that told intricate stories. Her mind was a library, and she stored everything she had ever seen, ever read or known, here on marvelous display. Exotic animals wandered past statuaries and famous works of art. I nearly got lost just looking around. Nessa was waiting for me out on an expansive lanai that overlooked a massive plunging waterfall. She was at the edge of the lanai, leaning on the gold banister, admiring at the horizon—her horizon—tall blue mountains going on as far as I could see.

She looked much younger than she really was, around my age, in fact, and she wore a long white gauzy gown. She was beautiful, no other word to explain it. She turned to me, smiled, and then motioned me over.

"You need to think better of yourself, Charlie boy," she said, her voice still the voice of years. "Get some skin on those bones."

I looked at my arms. I was still a skeleton.

"After all," she continued, "you might be the first person I ever met who can wake the dead. That's a true talent."

I was puzzled by this statement.

"The spirits in the house, the ones that's stuck there filthin' up the place, they're startin' to wake. I can feel it, sure. That's because of you, Charlie."

"You *are* a witch, ain't you?" I said. I didn't mean for it to come out so blunt. "You told me once that you wasn't a witch, but you are so. How else would you know about glamours and ghosts?"

"Just because I learned a few tricks from my mama don't make me a witch. It just makes me attentive. You learnt from Leroy how to fry an egg. Does that make you a chef? No, it does not. I listened good to my mama, and she left behind a wealth of information in books and notepads when she passed. That was my inheritance. Now, you best be followin' my example, boy. You need to pay attention." She stared me dead in the eye sockets. "I don't know how strong Jimmy's glamour is. It's holdin' off the shadow right now, sure, but a glamour weakens over time."

"Can't you just put a new one on him when that happens?"

"No, fool. You need to wake his ass up and get him out of here so I don't need to do that."

"He's comatose. How am I supposed to wake him up? You tell me."

"No. You tell me," she said, placing her hands on her hips and raising her eyebrows. I felt like I was being scolded by my mother. I'm near certain that was what it would feel like if I'd had one.

I huffed and looked around the lanai. It sure was pretty there: blue skies with clouds so fluffy I wanted to squeeze them. And birds too. Birds so big they might have been prehistoric. If I was Nessa and had an inner dream world like this, I'd stay in my dreams all the time. I'd never want to wake up. What's there to wake up to, anyway? She didn't have any family to… And that's when an idea hit me.

"It's Leroy," I said. "The only way to wake Jimmy up, the only way he's gonna live at all, is if Leroy is there with him."

"Now you gettin' it. And the only way for you to move on to the Evermore, Charlie boy, is to get them back together. They are your unfinished business."

"I know that," I said. "Don't you think I know that?"

"Well," she said, tapping her toes on the marble floor, "how you gonna go about gettin' it done, Mr. Smartass?"

Why did she care? I wondered. She had an ulterior motive for wanting Jimmy awake. I could sense that. Nessa was good at hiding many things, but when I was in her head, there was a whiff of anxiety in the air. I was sure I heard her brother's name being whispered in the breeze, too, but what Ray had to do with anything was lost on me.

"Possession," I said, thinking back on horror stories I had read. "What about possession?"

That made her uncomfortable. I saw her step back from me slightly. "You wanna possess Jimmy?"

"It would get him up, wouldn't it? It would get him out of here. I could take control of his body long enough to get him to Leroy's. He'd be where he's supposed to be and away from the shadow man and Bull."

She studied me a moment. "From what I learned from Mama, possession ain't an easy task. It takes a lot of focus and energy. It can wipe both the spirit and the vessel out. I wouldn't recommend it. Jimmy's a big boy. You'd never be able to do it."

Whispers, excited and rushed, filled the air. Nessa seemed to gain control of herself, though, and they hushed.

She was thinking, coming up with something behind the curtains, so to speak. She liked my idea.

"Might work, though," she said. "If you worked yourself up to Jimmy, started with small animals first so you could gain some strength, it might be possible."

"Would he fight me?" I asked. "I don't want to violate him. I don't want him to feel like I felt when the shadow man tried to take me. That was awful, Miss Nessa."

"You need to ask him, Charlie boy." She was stifling a grin, and as her eyes left my face and wandered off to the backdrop of her own head, I could hear the whispers rush back like falling water. "Yes," she said in a quieter voice. "This might work. But you need to be absolute certain why you want to possess him."

"For Leroy," I said. "Why else would I want to possess Jimmy?"

She looked at me and took a deep breath. "Charlie," she said, "I don't think you know why you really want to do this, and that can be dangerous."

If my sockets had eyes, I would have rolled them at the crazy bitch. But then she would have smacked me.

"Just tell me how to do it."

She shrugged. "I ain't a spirit," she said, leaning back over the banister. "But I'm guessin' it might be as easy as slippin' on a coat."

Nessa decided to take her leave soon after, and the whole beautiful landscape of her mind dissolved into the overgrown garden in an instant. I had been escorted out and was standing in the middle of chickens. Before I realized what was happening, I saw Nessa—the older version—with her burlap sack over her shoulder, walking off into the woods.

Back in the house, I was gonna try and get into Jimmy's head again, maybe ask him about the whole possessing issue. I was still trying to work out how I would bring it up when I noticed his empty bed. The covers had been thrown off and, momentarily, so had I. My immediate thought was that maybe the glamour didn't work. Maybe Jimmy had been dragged off by the shadow man to some hell while I was out talking to Nessa. The grays could offer me no answers. They were still bumbling around, mindless and dull, and I cursed them for it.

As I prepared at once to search the house from basement to attic for Jimmy, I heard the flush of the toilet. Jimmy then came stumbling out of the small half-bathroom under the stairs. I was so relieved and shocked, I didn't move as he passed right through me. Part of me wanted to grab onto him, to see if I could slip into him right there. But I didn't. I just watched him climb back into the bed and pull the covers over his head. He was in his bone house, and it was gonna take a lot for me to talk him out of it. Still, he was going to the bathroom on his own. That was a good sign.

Realizing I needed to get started immediately, I made my way outside, and boy, did I ever go on a trip. I figured I'd get right into it, no dillying or dallying, and try doing some possessions. Nessa was right. It wasn't very hard at all to get into another creature's physical form. I just had to say to the critter, *Listen, critter, I'm gonna take over your body for a bit, just a bit, and I promise I'll give it back to you unharmed. Sure, it might be a little scary, but it's for a good cause.* Then, as long as they didn't run, I'd burrow on in like a mole in a hole. You wouldn't think a soul as big as mine would fit into a rabbit or a squirrel, but then, in truth, I really ain't much but air and consciousness anymore. I just poured myself right on in, every bit of me, until I was looking out through a confused critter's eyes.

I'll admit, I was too big for some. Ain't no way all the soul of a man gonna fit into the body of a tiny field mouse. Wonder if Mr. Steinbeck knew that? And there were some birds—sweet little sparrows and the like—I wasn't gonna try to climb into either. The poor miniature things might have heart attacks and die while I was in them, and I wasn't certain if I'd be able to get back out after that. I kept to the larger forest creatures and birds. I was looking forward to being in flight while possessing a hawk. I've never flown on a plane, and I've always wanted to see things from up there. But once I finally managed inside of one, he wouldn't take to the air. Guess he sensed something was off. I wasn't strong enough yet to actually take over his body, so it's not like I could make him fly myself. And even if I had that ability, I wouldn't have done it. I don't know how to fly.

The little fluffy ground critters were fidgety. They were always scared that something was just behind a tree or a bush looking to make a snack of them. While hawks were on the lookout for teeth or guns, rabbits were on the lookout for talons or teeth. I didn't stay in any animal for too long lest I get eaten by a coyote or a fox. I even tried to possess a coyote, but he was too wily for me. Being of the canine family, he was aware of my presence at all times, even if he couldn't see me.

I kept up the possessing game for hours. I didn't need sleep, after all, and the little fellas, being so small, weren't tiring me out. Soon I found I was even able to wiggle my ear when I was a rabbit. Taking over these little furry bodies was easy enough, sure. But what about a big furry body who didn't want to do a damn thing but lay around? To ready myself for that, I tried possessing a tree, a big twisted oak by the creek in the woods. It wasn't too happy; in fact, it was downright grumpy, but I had asked, after all. Not my fault it didn't reply. Being in a tree's skin is peculiar.

You're vulnerable and imposing at once. You're a complete ecosystem, housing all types of bugs, moss, and downy things, some of them truly disgusting. And you don't see the world as much as you feel it. Truth is, I had no sight as a tree. Not really. Just an impression of the forest around me. After a few minutes, I decided to leave the tree be. It seemed a very dull existence. Besides, I couldn't make a tree walk. I didn't have the strength. Yet.

When I was done, finished possessing the woodland critters for the time being, I carefully climbed out of a raccoon and watched it scurry away, perhaps a bit confused but none the worse for my wear. I looked back at the caretaker's house and, to my utter surprise, saw the porch was crowded with grays. Not all of them, mind you, but enough to make me a bit anxious. Cal was at the forefront of the lot, on the steps, the whites of his eyes nearly glowing. Others, who now seemed to be waking up as well, stood behind him. They were all staring at me like they couldn't see so good in the dark.

"Neat trick." Alfie was behind me. He came walking up out of the woods leisurely, hands once again in pockets. "They don't understand what you're up to." He nodded to the grays. "But they wanna know. You're the best show in town these days, Charlie."

"You're back," I said. "I didn't think you'd ever come back."

"I ain't smart enough to stay away." He walked up alongside me. "Besides, maybe this is my unfinished business. Maybe after I deal with that house I can move on to whatever comes next. Guess what I'm sayin' is, I'll help you out." He smirked and leaned towards me. "It's all entirely selfish on my part." He nodded to Cal. "The old animal trainer is wide awake now. The other normals are gettin' there, too, it seems. Let's hope the shadow man don't notice."

"So, yeah. I'll help you, if you need me," he said as we walked to the porch. "Wake your friend, I mean. I'll help you, though I don't know what I could do."

"I appreciate it just the same," I replied.

It was a bit startling having to go up the steps and into the caretaker's house surrounded by the grays, especially Cal. He was such a tall, dead-looking thing, and behind that face of death there was most certainly a consciousness. He did not look like he had been a happy man in life or a happy ghost in death, yet I could tell he was listening to every word I said, and not only that, he understood most of them.

Me and Alfie sat on Jimmy's bed. "I need to slip into Jimmy's head," I said. "It's best I do it now while I still got the energy. Watch him, would you? I'll climb back out the first sign of trouble."

He was looking at me like I was crazy. "How you plan on gettin' in there? I told ya I don't know anything about gettin' into a man's head."

"The basement, silly."

He stared at me, baffled, but remained there on the bed next to Jimmy.

Jimmy's bone house was repairing itself as I stepped inside. This time I entered on my first step down into the basement. I saw the dusty bone banisters lifting and healing themselves from the damage done to them by the shadow man. Looking over the edge, I heard the echoes of repair all the way down, the knocking of bone against bone, a hollow sort of reunion that only amplified the desperate loneliness of Jimmy's inner self.

I found Jimmy in much the same condition as when I had left him. He was still old and withered and still clinging to the bed.

"You can let go now," I assured him, coming down from the staircase. "The darkness is gone."

"Oh no," he replied. "The darkness is all around. It never leaves, just changes form. It's always underneath or behind the walls. It waits to eat us up, every one of us. We're all just bidin' our time until we're on the dinner table. It has a name, you know. Darkness is Love."

I squatted in front of him, still a skeleton. "I need to ask a favor of you, Jimmy," I said. "Can you do me a favor? It's for both of us. All three of us, in fact. You, me, and Leroy."

"Leroy?" His eyes met mine.

"Yeah, for Leroy. Now this is gonna sound strange, so I'm just gonna come out with it. I need to borrow your body, Jimmy. I need to get inside it, to possess it for a bit. Would that be okay?"

He took such a long time to respond that I was certain he was gonna say no.

But then with a deep breath, he said with a shrug, "Why not? I ain't usin' it."

"You see, that's just it, Jimmy. I'm gonna make it so you're gonna use it again. I'm gonna reunite you with Leroy. Won't that be something?"

"Why did he leave me?" he moaned as he fell back on the bed. His whispers grew loud and piteous, and I knew there wasn't going to be any more talking. At least not from Jimmy.

I emerged from the basement, and the grays were in the parlor with Alfie and Jimmy, a house full of the dead waiting on the living.

"Well?" Alfie asked, rising to his feet. "Did you get done what you needed to do?"

"He's gonna let me do it," I said. "He's gonna let me possess him. But I don't think he really understands what I intend to do."

"Do we need to prepare the body somehow? Is there some ritual we should do?"

"No. But I do need to practice a bit more. Jimmy's a big boy. Bigger than a damn rabbit, that's for sure."

"Let's get to it, then," said Alfie. "Them woods is filled with deer and wild pigs. Might even be a bear in there."

* * * *

Possessing form after being without one for some time is a bit constraining, like putting on a coat that's two sizes too small. Added to that, it's some other soul's body. You're just borrowing it for a while. It wasn't made for you, so of course it's gonna feel strange. It'll never fit perfectly.

The next day me and Alfie were in the woods hunting. Alfie was gonna watch out for me once we found the appropriate animal for me to possess and make certain I didn't get attacked by a bobcat or even a wolf while I was inside. Hunting was not a difficult thing. We found a wild pig pretty quick, and I was able to slip beneath its blubber without it giving so much as a squeal. I found I was actually pretty good at this whole possession thing. I had that oinker walking around the woods in no time. Alfie followed me close behind.

"Heh," Alfie laughed. "You look like my cock did, all fat and hairless."

And then, I don't know whether it was from wanting to fill the silent air with words or just wanting to finally tell his tale, Alfie told me what had happened to him:

"You see," he began, his hands in his pockets as he scuffled behind me, "I was born with an enormous dick. Nice length, I suppose, around eight inches, but thicker and heavier than the average wiener. When it wasn't erect it looked like a big squat bullfrog, heh, or a little baby pig. I never had sex. Not ever. It wouldn't fit into no one's hole, woman or man. It was a real nuisance, to be honest. I couldn't let myself get excited around people because it was a monster, and I couldn't take a shit without my balls fallin' into the toilet water. I had to tape him to my belly at times.

"I was put in the midnight show with a few of the other freaks who wasn't meant to be seen by children or the weak of heart. During the day, I worked around the carnival doin' maintenance shit, but at night, I was a star. I was made to do some awful things with my monster. It was do as I was told or leave. My body belonged to the carnival. I even had to act the part, you know. Like I was a sex-crazed psychopath and the circus was actually doin' a civic duty by keepin' me locked up, makin' sure I wasn't out rapin' boys and girls and destroyin' the world's assholes. But there ain't no way I could destroy all the world's assholes cause there's more of 'em born every minute.

"The fact that I couldn't put my monster up in anyone didn't mean I didn't have a romantic life, though. I had me a fella, the circus strongman. He was a real sweet guy the same age as me who loved music. My lord, could he play too! And he weight trained to classical stuff, lifting to violins and doin' squats to symphonies. Where I had been blessed with an over-abundance of cock, my poor strongman had just the opposite problem. But that didn't matter. He liked me and I liked him. It's good to have somebody, you know, so the hours don't feel so long and cold. Me and my strongman, we spent many a night together, rubbin' on each other, lovin' on each other. I don't know if we made each other happy, but we sure made each other content. Until Flora, that is.

"Flora was a normal, as I've told ya, and freaks and normals never said word one to each other. Those were the unspoken rules. But Flora didn't care about the rules, and she was so damn beautiful she could get away with not carin'. She had long wavy black hair that seemed to curl around her shoulders and waist like it was molestin' her. Shit, she could do whatever she wanted to do and smile doing it. Some of the normals even hated her for that. That there was a gal who got what she wanted. Well, with one look at me and my monster one night, I guess she decided I was next on her to-do list. She started bein' all friendly with me, laughin' at my feeble attempts at jokes. My strongman saw through her better than me. 'Alfie,' he said, 'don't you trust her! She's tryin' to come between us.' But I didn't believe him. She just needed a friend. What would such a beauty want with me? Certainly wasn't my sexual prowess. She'd seen my midnight shows and the acts I had to perform, and I had seen the look of disgust on her face.

"Still, one night after a show, she came backstage and straddled me while I was still naked and sticky. She made me hard, I'll admit it, rubbin' me up and down. But my monster couldn't do anything for her unless she wanted a useless pussy the rest of her life. She bounced up and down on me just the same, makin' me feel good till I splooged all over the place. That's when I saw my strongman. I don't know how long he'd been watchin', but the look on his face told me all I needed to know about how he was feelin'.

"I hurried and got cleaned up and dressed, hopin' to clear things up between me and him, but when I got back to our rack, he was gone and so was everything he owned. Poor Carter done left me, and I never had a chance to explain."

It was the blindside of hearing my killer's name that knocked me out of the pig and onto the forest floor. The pig ran off squealing into the brush. Carter? Could it be the same man, the very same violinist? He was a man of some fifty years now, if so, though still a strongman in many ways. Strange that he hadn't gone too far away from the carnival to try and make a better life for himself.

"You okay, Charlie?" Alfie asked, staring at me, almost concerned.

"Yeah," I said, picking myself up. "I'm fine. How'd I do in that pig?"

"You looked like a pig to me, and I've seen a lot of pigs. You done real good."

The next day I decided to find an animal with more speed and agility. I needed to be faster than a pig if I was gonna possess a grown man. We found a young buck deer grazing in the woods, and while I was sprinting clumsily through the trees, Alfie continued his story:

"Of course, I missed my strongman," said Alfie as he kept up with me no problem. "I'll admit that right now. I truly missed him. Still do, I suppose. He was the sweetest fella I ever met. I never heard him raise his voice once. Not at me, at least. But Flora had some strange hold on me. I can't say it was witchcraft, and I can't say it was love. It was more like I was watchin' a show and I wanted to see how it all ended.

"Well, as you now know by my bein' here talkin' to you, it ended bad. Real bad. I should have known somethin' was wrong the night I saw her talkin' to the caretaker behind the haunted house. No one ever talked to the caretaker but the higher-ups, and even they stayed away from him unless they was called. The caretaker, well, there was a disturbin' man, for certain. He was always watchin' from the shadows and as tall as…well, you seen him. He's still in that house. At least part of him is. The darkest part. When I saw him with Flora, I got the stone-cold chills. That was the first time I ever saw his nerve-damaged face. In the sparse light, it flipped and jumped like you never thought eyes and lips was supposed to. There was rumors he had been a doctor of some sort once, but no one ever knew for sure. Maybe he had messed up his face by inhalin' too much nerve gas that was meant for his patients. Flora wouldn't even look at him directly. She just nodded her head whenever he said somethin' in that desolate whisper voice he had. Lawd, that voice was unhinged. She looked like a baby girl bein' lectured by the devil himself in that light. I didn't stay much longer, nor did I hear anything that was said. I snuck away and promised myself that I would avoid Flora after that. She was messin' with the wrong sort of folk, I thought. How was I to know that the caretaker was her daddy and she didn't really have a choice in the matter?"

I climbed out of the young buck a bit drained of energy. "The caretaker had a daughter?" I said.

"Sure did. It's a shame you can't pick your family, huh?"

"Sure you can," I replied. It was a realization that just came to me. "How'd I do?" I asked, glancing over to the buck that still stood nearby, confused and innocent.

"A little drunk," Alfie replied. "But you was a deer. I would have proudly shot ya and hung you on my wall, myself. Good job."

The next day I was able to find me an unsuspecting wolf. He was a pretty thing, black and fierce. He must have been the slow one in the pack, though, because while the others whooped and ran once they sensed me, he paused just long enough for me to burrow inside. I felt more comfortable in him than in any of the animals I had possessed so far. He nearly fit.

"After a few days," continued Alfie as I prowled the forest in my new form, "I thought Flora had run away. I didn't see her no more, not even when there was a show. I'm ashamed to say I looked for her too. I missed the attention, however misguided and cruel. Now without her or my strongman, I was so deadly lonesome I wanted to cry. You see, I was never freak enough to be considered one of them—my cock was hidden in my pants. But on the flip side, I was never normal enough to be with them—there was clearly a massive cock in my pants. I was on my own.

"Then one night, I was woke up by a cryin' outside my quarters. It was Flora, and she looked a mess, like she'd been beaten and dragged through the mud. 'Who did this to you?' I asked. She looked up at me, and man, she had been a good actress because I noticed then and too late that her eyes were as dry as mine. She'd just been sobbin' to get me to come outside in the middle of the night. The grin she gave me resembled her daddy's, and then everything went dark. I had been hit on the back of the head and clean knocked out.

"I woke up to a throbbin' head, and that wasn't helped none by high-pitched screams. Not my own screams, though. These was Flora's. Once my vision returned to me, I perceived I was in a cage, a small metal one for a dog or somethin', in the attic of that very house your friend now sleeps in. Of course, I didn't know that's where I was at the time. Only after I died was I able to see my whereabouts clearly. What I did know and could see, though, was that I was in deep shit. I was naked and cold. I twisted my head around, and I saw Flora strapped to a table. She was cryin' and shakin' at the caretaker, screamin' at him. He was cuttin' into her this way then that, but never cuttin' too deep. It was clear he was just playin' around for the moment. 'You promised, Daddy,' she screamed. 'You promised you'd let me go if I brought you the sexual deviant. You promised!'

"But her daddy didn't say anything. He just grinned in his strange, contorted manner and carved on like she was a damn turkey. Her screams were awful, just nightmarish things. I couldn't take 'em anymore, so I shouted out, 'Hey! That's your girl! What kind of daddy are you? Leave her alone.'

"The caretaker looked up at me like he just realized I was there. It was the coldest look I ever received from anybody in all my life. Not even the normals looked at me like that. You know, Charlie, people will tell you that the opposite of love is hate, but that ain't true. No, the opposite of love is indifference; it's apathy. The caretaker took a broad knife from the table beside him that held such things, and he plunged it deep into Flora's chest. She seized and struggled for a few seconds, and then her face rolled to the side, as dumb and numb as you please. There wasn't a hint of anguish on that pretty face no more, just a trickle of blood comin' up out of her mouth and drippin' from those pouty lips.

"After that…well, I became the caretaker's choice plaything for a while. I was kept in that cage until he decided it gave me too much room and so he put me into a smaller cage. He did some awful things to me, Charlie. Some truly horrible…"

By this time, I had climbed out of the wolf and let it rejoin the pack. I was sitting high on a tree branch with Alfie, listening to his tale, waiting for him to go on. It was a while before he collected himself.

"But thankfully," he finally spoke, "in time, he found somethin' else to entertain him, and I was killed. A few years later, he was found out. A young boy who he had plans to turn into a lampshade escaped and told the cops all that he'd seen. The caretaker didn't know what was happenin' when the police converged on the house. Too late for me, though. Too late for a whole bunch of us. He killed close to fifty people in all, circus folk, freaks and normals. None of us ever had much of a life, but still, they were our lives not to have, you know?"

I put my hand in his.

"Was you murdered too, Charlie?" he asked me.

"I was," I told him.

"Is your killer still alive? Is he still out walkin' amongst the livin'?"

"He is."

"You should find a way to kill the bastard," he said. "Else you ain't never gonna move on. That's what I think, anyway. That's why most of us can't move on from here. The guy who killed us is long gone, shot by the cops who came for him, and the shadow he left behind is indestructible."

We sat there for some time, not saying a word.

Alfie's words about the caretaker stuck in my head. Indestructible, maybe. But not invincible. The shadow man couldn't even get close to Jimmy now that Nessa had given him a glamour. As long as that glamour stayed strong, Jimmy was safe. And, dammit, if Nessa could tell that old shadow man to fuck off, I could too. I just needed to find out how, was all.

* * * *

Well, that conversation with Alfie woke something mean in me. I needed to see my killer again, to wreak some sort of vengeance on him. Alfie was right. It was my life to screw up, and Carter had taken it from me. It wasn't a great life by any means, but it was all I knew and it belonged to me. It was the only thing in this whole wide world that was indisputably mine.

That night I stood outside Nessa's shack in the woods. I knew she wouldn't come out and greet me. Hell, she wouldn't even come to the door. But she would sense I was there and would know that I needed something from her. So I stared down the shack, oblivious to any passing souls or elementals that might also be in the woods around me. This time I wasn't even gonna need to get into Nessa's head. I needed her help in another, much more physical way.

I went back to the caretaker's house after a few hours, after I was certain my point had been made, and I slipped into Jimmy's body. The grays watched with startled expressions that I found more unnerving than their blank stares. Maybe I was being a bad influence on them. Maybe they would think they could do this possession thing, too, and not just to Jimmy. But I didn't have time to worry about that. Besides, Jimmy had his glamour that protected him from everyone but me. Everybody else in the world was on their own. If they didn't want ghosts possessing them, well, then call a damn exorcist, for all the good it would do.

Having a body again, a real human body with a pulse, was goddamn exhilarating. I could feel Jimmy's extremities, his arms, his legs, his cock, in a sort of tingling numb way, like they'd all fallen asleep and were just now waking back up. And it hit me, blood flow. I have blood flow. Liquid blood is a heavy thing when you're made of air and consciousness. It's a delicious heaviness, though. Goddamn those vampires. I could feel his lungs filled with oxygen, and I took a deep breath.

"Hey, Charlie boy," I heard his voice inside of him—inside of me—calmly say.

I responded with "Hey there, Jimmy. Do you mind if I take you for a ride?"

"Go ahead," he replied. "I'm gonna take a nap."

I couldn't see the grays anymore as I made my way, clumsily at first, to the bathroom mirror. (I very well might have walked right through Cal. He was standing nearest the bed when I possessed Jimmy.) It's strange looking at yourself wearing someone else's face. Kind of horrifying, actually. I recognized the flash in Jimmy's otherwise dulled eyes as me, but the rugged unshaven face as pale as handsome death, that was all Jimmy. I rubbed at his face, feeling actual flesh for the first time in a while. That was something else. Warm chills, how I missed them. They made me smile—on the inside. I couldn't make the face I wore smile, though, no matter how hard I tried. For all intents and purposes, Jimmy was a zombie.

I spent some time in Jimmy's body, getting use to its quirks, using the bathroom (I had forgotten about the often urgent reminders from human plumbing), eating something (because I knew Jimmy had not been taking care of his nutritional needs), and basically learning to walk again with real legs. Balance is a tricky bitch. When a knock came at the door at dawn, I initially forgot I could go answer it.

It took three knocks and Nessa yelling, "Charlie! Jimmy! You in there?" for me to realize, *Oh yeah! I invited her.*

The first thing she said as I opened the door and she looked into Jimmy's eyes was "Jesus Christ…"

"Close enough," I said in Jimmy's voice. Like the rest of the man, Jimmy's voice was a heavy thing, so when I spoke, it sounded like a serial killer's whisper. "Can you take me to Devlin?"

She drove the blue land yacht in silence, with me looking at her a good portion of the way. Seeing through Jimmy's eyes was like needing glasses. Everything I now knew as a dead boy was in the air, all the elementals and beautiful color shades that could never be described with words, were suddenly gone, as was the shimmering glamour that I knew still surrounded Nessa.

I was staring at her, in fact, with what must have been the cocked confused face of a dog, when she said, "You need to stop lookin' at me, Charlie boy. You creepin' me out, ya hear? I'll help ya out, and I know you doin' this for Jimmy's own good, but ya need to rein yourself in and act like ya got a bit of normal, okay?"

"Yes, ma'am," I said. "Sorry, Miss Nessa."

She waited in the Buick when we reached Carter's rundown apartment building. I got out of the car and stared up at the window on the second floor, the room I had been killed in. I took Nessa's advice. I got myself a bit of normal and strode into the building. I didn't know what I was gonna do when I saw him. I could kill him, that's true. Or I could just give him a big scare. Or I could fuck him dead like he did me. He took something that belonged to me, after all. The biggest something there is, I suppose. I could say to him as he opened the door, "I'm gonna fucking kill you," and it would be the honest truth in every way.

The door was unlocked when I got to his apartment, so I let myself in and was immediately set upon by the foul funk of someone who's done let themselves go. That was how Jimmy was gonna start smelling if he didn't start washing himself, especially with these end-of-summer days being so damn hot. Carter was lying passed out on the floor beside his bed, naked but for a pair of stained underwear. He was a mess. He was still half grasping an empty bottle of

Jack Daniel's. Regret congealed on his chin in the form of slobber. If this was remorse for killing me, it did nothing to distract me from my purpose. The violin I had heard him play at Patricia's little gathering where I'd met him lay scattered in pieces all over the floor.

I leaned nearer to him, doing my best to keep my balance, and looked on his perhaps once-handsome face. If this was Alfie's strongman, I couldn't see it. There was no youth there, only years and years of pain attached to a body that grew bigger as his heart shrank. There was still liquor in his mouth he had yet to swallow. It was dribbling out in a sticky stream. I reached for his thick neck, to give it a squeeze, to see him struggle the way he had made me struggle. To see that vein gorge to the point of bursting.

Then he suddenly spoke a word while he slept, spewing a bit of the alcohol still in his mouth.

"Alfie."

He said it with such love and regret that my hand—Jimmy's hand—fell slack to my side. Here was a man who, like me, had been tossed away, thinking nobody in the world loved him. He was a killer, no doubt. But there was an innocence to him, still. How could I harm him? Aside from that, how could I let Jimmy take the rap for his murder? Because, sure as hell, there would be fingerprints, and they wouldn't be mine. I wanted revenge. I did. But I couldn't take it.

Yet as I squatted there in front of Carter the violinist, Carter the strongman, Carter the killer, he said Alfie's name once more. Only this time, the remaining liquor in his mouth must have slid down his throat, and he began to choke. He turned awful savage colors, mean and angry shades of purple, and he started to convulse. It was a horrific thing to see, but also satisfying. Maybe I should have helped him. Maybe I should have woken him up and saved his life. But that wasn't what I had come here for.

Instead, I stood and stared down at him a moment more as he continued to gasp for air, so inebriated there was no hope for him to wake up on his own. I left before Carter saw his Death. It did not escape me that Carter's Death might, in fact, be my image since I was most likely the last person to show him any affection at all, even if it was paid for. I wondered if he would be terrified by this or relieved. I wondered if he would scream or beg for forgiveness. Of course, I wouldn't be able to hear him if I had stayed to watch him breathe his last. Not through Jimmy's ears anyway.

Nessa was waiting for me in the car. "Did ya do what ya needed to?" she asked. Her eyes were boring into me like she knew what I had planned to do. Somehow, though, I knew she was not above a little vengeance, nor would she hold my need for retribution against me. We were peas in a big blue Buick-shaped pod.

"Yes, ma'am," I said. "You can take me home now. Thank you."

I was getting tired. Holding on to Jimmy's form was wiping me out. Possessing something is a bit like holding your hands up in the air. After a while, you just can't do it no more. The sky gets heavy.

Night was falling when we arrived back at the caretaker's house. In the dusk light, Nessa saw Bull's truck in front before I did, and she pulled over and turned off the ignition and the lights. My vision through Jimmy's eyes was getting hazy, but I knew the shape of Bull's monster.

"Stay in the car," Nessa said as she opened the door and walked cautiously to the house. I wanted to go with her, but to burrow out of Jimmy's body and leave him there alone would have been stupid. Besides, I was exhausted. I didn't recall being that exhausted even when I was alive. Being alive again was killing me. If I had followed her, I don't know if I could have made it into the house.

And then, stepping out of the dark, there was Bull. Him and his dog were standing directly in front of the car and that man had a smirk on his face as mean and lopsided as a homicidal Siamese twin. Lighting a match, he took a step towards the car. I wasn't about to let Jimmy be incinerated alive like I had Trent, so I pulled up all my strength and got out of the car, slowly, unbothered, my eyes never losing contact with Bull. At this point, Dog sensed something about me, about Jimmy. His ears pricked up, and he started growling, but not in the way he had been. He was frightened now. Bull noticed it, but the peculiarity only gave him slight pause. Dog ran off into the woods, but Bull came at me even as I stumbled backwards and took a hard fall to the ground.

The impact of Jimmy's body hitting the ground knocked me loose of him, his flesh finally too heavy, and I tumbled out a few feet away. I watched in horror, unable to do a thing, as Bull approached Jimmy, who now lay unconscious by the car. I tried crawling back to Jimmy, but I was not going to make it. That would be two people I had delivered into the fires. I started calling to Jimmy, screaming at him to wake up. Bull's eyes were two mirror images of the flame he held in his hand. If there was a devil, that is what he looked like, large, grinning, and with eyes of fire.

A loud conk broke the tension in the night air, however, and Bull dropped his match to the ground and fell sideways. Nessa stood right behind him with a shovel from the garage. Bull rose, dazed and unable to see Nessa because of the glamour. But he could hear her.

"Get outta here!" she yelled. There was something in her eyes, like she was holding back. Like she wanted to beat Bull into the ground. Vengeance.

To Bull it must have seemed like a banshee in the night, because he looked around with that same expression he had when I got pissed at him in the caretaker's house and started throwing shit. Holding the back of his head, he got into his truck and drove off crookedly and drunk.

Nessa was on the ground holding Jimmy. I had managed to crawl up beside them. "Ya need to get Jimmy out of here and fast," she said to me. "The house is trashed, and Bull will be back. He got a dark spirit inside of him, dark and smelly as Satan's shit. There ain't one thing that'll ever quell a dark spirit, Charlie boy."

We sat there on the gravel road for a while. I suppose all of us needed some time to recuperate, and there was as good a place as any. I wasn't certain if I was ever gonna be able to walk again at first. I was so pained. Let me tell you, there ain't nothing final about death. When you die, you just end up in another existence, one that comes with its own pains and exhaustions. It's some big cosmic joke, I guess.

"Remember I was tellin' you once about my brother Ray?" Nessa asked after some time, still cradling Jimmy. "It was Bull who killt him. The very same devil who killt your friend killt my brother. Ray was dead long before I came lookin' for him. But I know'd it was Bull who done it. I saw it in a dream, like you did of your friend. Bull burnt Ray alive like he was some trash or shit. My brother gone on now, gone to the next place, wherever that is, but I can't leave this world until I make Bull pay. Every night, I dream and I see my brother's anguished face, his…his awful, truly awful, screams. And for that, Bull gonna pay. I coulda done it tonight. Coulda killt him right here. But I want that asshole to pay more dearly than a couple of shovel knocks to the head will do. I whittled me some sticks into spears. You seen 'em back at my place. They'd be mighty painful stuck in his eyes, or even up his ass. But they ain't enough. The pain they'd inflict would be over much too soon. I see that now. Nah, for our Bull, we need somethin' lastin', somethin' forever dreadful." She looked at me then—right at me— though I know she couldn't see me. "You know what I'm sayin' to ya, Charlie boy?"

* * * *

The next day, though I was plum tuckered out from wearing Jimmy, Alfie and me went into the woods to see if there was something that might let me possess it, even for a bit. After a wee squirrel was able to run away from my approach, though, I figured I was pretty much done for the day. Besides, I knew I could handle a squirrel. What I needed was more human practice. I know it sounds creepy, me saying that. I hear it myself. I'd become the boogeyman.

"Too bad these woods ain't crawling with runaways," said Alfie. "You'd get all the practice you wanted with some meth-addicted runaways."

"Naw," I said. "I wouldn't possess a runaway. They would have had a hard life already without some spirit taking control of their body. Humans are delicate things, anyway, runaways even more so. Maybe that don't show on the exterior, how fragile they are. But on the inside, there's a need for acceptance that barely keeps them hanging together, limb to limb, tendon to tendon. At least, that's how it was with me. I can say that now without blushing."

"Everybody needs love. That's true enough. But it's such a hard thing to find." We stopped at the burnt-down carnival gate. Alfie kicked at a pile of ash, and a small black storm rose into the air. "We fall to pieces for love. Or we're torn apart by it. Just torn apart."

His eyes were staring off at the decrepit buildings and debris of some forced past happiness. That's what carnivals are, after all, a way to force yourself to be happy even if you're feeling like shit.

"I wanna show you somethin', Charlie," Alfie said in a voice that was drowned in a whisper.

I followed him past all the amusements, the abandonments, and the torments to the fun house. The fun house and the haunted house were two different places, the fun house being a once-brightly colored place—now only slightly colored yellow—filled with mirrors and wackiness, and the haunted house…well, that don't need no more explaining.

Inside, we walked past the fun-house ruins, broken mirrors and topsy-turvy rooms, until we came to a door marked 'For Employees Only.' We went down a stairs that was only half there and into old darkness. Alfie remained silent the whole time, not saying a word. He glowed in sepia, like nostalgia. The basement was filled with junk and unused fun-house attractions. But at the far end, in a corner tucked away from everything, was a large caged area marked 'For the Caretaker Only.' Inside of that was rows of glass tanks, some of them was cracked and broken, others were filled with a thick dark green fluid. Some had dead animals in them, squirrels and possums, but most were empty of anything but the green.

Then my eyes flew wide. There was a series of glass tanks I found most disturbing. The first contained a pair of human legs, young legs, like mine, the strong thighs leaning against the glass. The next had a pair of human arms, the hands and fingers posed almost artistically. And then, by the third tank, I realized what Alfie had brought in me there for, because in that tank was an abnormally large-sized cock and balls pressed up against the glass like they was trying to get out. I didn't want to see no farther, but I could not deny my friend the closest thing to a funeral he would ever have. Finally, in the last tank, there was the torso and head of a young man, of Alfie, eyes and mouth wide open, caught in a scream. I could not help but gasp as if grasping for air.

"This is what the caretaker did to me," said Alfie, his voice now a shaking murmur. "After he killed Flora, he spent most of his time the next few weeks torturin' me. He kept me alive in the cage, but every few days, I would wake up from a deep sleep with somethin' missin'—an arm, then my legs, and finally he took my cock. I was just a miserable stump in the attic for a couple of days until he decided to kill me. He fucked me one last time, and then he strangled me, but I was dead long before that, I think." Alfie turned to me. "I just thought you should know, Charlie. I thought you should see what the caretaker, the shadow man, was capable of. Some people ain't born with souls. All they got is flesh with darkness inside of it. And I ain't seen the light defeat the dark once in all this time. Not once."

* * * *

A few days later, I saw some improvement in Jimmy. He was getting up more, walking around, if aimlessly, but he still slept quite a bit. If he wasn't sleeping, he was just lying there, most likely thinking desolate thoughts.

From the confrontation with Bull, it was evident that Nessa's glamour on Jimmy was only working to keep the shadow man away. Bull's intent to harm Jimmy was too strong. Nessa said she'd be over to strengthen the glamour, but she didn't know if it would do any good. Some devils gotta be devilin', and their devilin' is just too fierce for the light.

I was sitting by Jimmy's bed. He was asleep, tossing and mumbling to and for Leroy. The house was quiet and dark, all the lights were off. Somewhere in here, behind a door or a wall, the shadow man was lurking about, but I tried not to think about him. Every sudden noise, every bump or creak, and I sat up straighter. But I wasn't gonna leave Jimmy's side.

Most of the grays were no longer milling about. Some sat still on the floor with their legs crossed, others examined their hands as if they were brand new to them, and still others—and this is the creepiest bit—they decided to try and speak. All that came out, though, was garbled dead talk that would have been enough to give me the prickly hairs if I still had hair. It sounded like somebody was having a butcher knife crammed down their throat. So I was already on edge. And then…

Before the door was busted open, I heard that ugly dog barking. It was a vicious but scared shitless yelping, and when Bull stood in the doorway, the door broken from its hinges and lying to the side, the dog remained outside. The grays who had tried to speak began moaning, groaning like a pack of coyotes. Bull couldn't hear them, of course, and if he did, he wasn't bothered by those old haunts. Devils ain't scared of gray ghosts. He looked in Jimmy's direction and grinned.

"Alone now, ain't ya, boy?" he said. "All alone now."

He started toward Jimmy so I flung everything I could at him, only this time that only served to agitate the bastard even more. He swatted at my defenses with big angry arms and continued to near my friend.

"Help me!" I screamed to the grays. "Help."

And to my surprise, they did. Watching how I did it, they joined in, throwing plates and pillows and anything they could find. Soon the parlor was a storm with debris flying through the air, all of it aimed at Bull. Still, it did not stop him. He merely swatted more feverishly and growled more ferociously.

As he reached Jimmy, I realized what I needed to do. *Practice makes perfect*, I thought. *Ain't gonna be a better specimen to practice on than ol' Bull.* So I plied open his karmic guard and burrowed into him as fiercely as I'd ever done. I felt the rush of confusion at once, his inner voice shouting at me, and I could feel the darkness inside of him, the absence of soul. But I had control now. I was Bull. I gripped to his flesh like I had talons, and I ran through that broken doorway. Once outside, I threw him on the ground near his whimpering dog. When I rolled out of him, I saw Nessa standing near us on top of my grave. She held one of the spears she had been whittling, and a look of absolute gaming concentration was on her face.

Bull was confused and agitated, and he rose again, stumbling but not deterred from his goal of killing Jimmy. He turned and made his way for the house. I looked at Nessa, who wasn't doing a damn thing. It was like she was waiting on something. I was tired but not exhausted. I could have burrowed into the giant stinking bastard again to keep him away from Jimmy and nearly did. The thing was, though, I didn't need to. The grays had followed me out of the house and were in the process of possessing all sorts of woodland critters—raccoons, rabbits, squirrels, owls. They had been watching me, after all. They had been learning, and were now burrowing deep into fur and guts. The possessions were instantaneous, and then they began to attack Bull, nipping at him, clawing and biting. The attack was almost comical if not for the gray shapes sinking in and out of the forest creatures like bubbling souls.

Dog was terrified, backing away and yelping as Bull was left on his own. Bull swatted at the raccoons as they sank their teeth into his shins and grabbed at the owls that went for his eyes. And then Dog, too, shushed his whining and began to growl, not at me or any of the other animals, but at Bull himself. Suddenly, as if on cue, the critters dispersed from around Bull, and he was left alone, bleeding but still on his feet. No sooner had this happened than Dog charged at his owner, felling him to the earth with a mighty *argh*. Bull cried out as Dog lay into him. Bull cursed the dog in agony as his cheek was torn clear off. Bull's body lay still as Dog ripped out the man's throat.

At this point, I was on my feet again and I saw all the risings. I saw the grays let go of their hold on the critters and remain standing around the yard; I saw Alfie climb out of Dog, who went yelping off into the woods; and I saw Bull's confused spirit standing over his bloodied corpse. Only it wasn't a spirit. No, Bull had no soul. What he was now was nothing more than a shimmering black mist in the shape of a man. He was a shadow. He howled as he looked around at all of us, but the grays paid him little mind. They slowly turned and walked back to the caretaker's house. He saw me then, probably recognized me, and a long black-as-tar hand reached for me, asking for some sort of explanation. I knew, though, if he touched me, it would only bring me pain.

"I see you!" shouted Nessa from atop my grave.

His attention was suddenly on her.

"I know you," she said with more hate and anger in her voice than I thought she was capable of. "You killt my brother. I see his torment every night."

He howled at her, racing to her now with frightening speed, his hand ready to rape her soul.

She smiled and let out a dry-as-ice chuckle. "May you never find peace, fool," she said. She thrust out her spear in a quick circular motion. A part of Bull, some dark tendril, became wrapped around the spear, and the more Nessa circled, the thicker that tendril became until it resembled a black chain. As Bull came upon her glamour, there was the crackle and hiss of an electric current and he screeched in anguish and fell to the ground.

"You are my dog now," she said. With one jerk of her spear, she began to pull him away like a dog on a chain, Bull screaming in the night, clawing at the ground, as he vanished into the woods with Nessa.

* * * *

I visited Nessa's shack not too long after that. Call it morbid curiosity. There wasn't a glamour over the place anymore. I suppose Nessa didn't feel she needed one now that Bull had been killed. She was on the porch, her feet resting up on a plastic bucket, while she stared off in the direction of what any other living person would see as no more than deep thought. Only a spirit could know that the satisfied grin on her face had nothing to do with some daydream or fantasy of the mind. No sir. Though she could not see him directly, she was staring right at Bull who she kept tied to her spear that was now driven deep into the forest ground. Bull was a-howling and a-thrashing, shimmering blackness and throwing shade even in the daylight. His leash would not give, though, never. Strangely enough, on the porch, sitting right beside Nessa just as calm as could be and only perking his ears every so often, was Dog. That hound didn't seem the same creature at all. All that meanness was gone, like maybe he just needed a good owner.

Bull saw me watching and roared. I flipped him off and left.

At the caretaker's house, Jimmy was sitting up. He still looked tired and beat all to hell, but at least he was moving around now. He had been totally oblivious to the danger he was in just a few nights before when Bull broke down the door. As far as concerns the shadow man, I hadn't heard or seen a wisp of him in a while. I knew he was there, though, waiting on something. The anticipation made my skin crawl.

Alfie was visiting the house more and more lately. It was almost like he preferred the house to the carnival. I was finding I did too. Alfie kept his eyes on Flora, the only gray in the caretaker's house to still be stumbling around numb and dumb, the only one who turned the other way when there was something to be learned.

"I'm tired of lookin' at her," Alfie said one afternoon. He had been sitting on a fainting chair, just watching her all day. He got up and took her by the hand, then led her up the stairs. I followed at a leisurely pace.

"What are you doing, Alfie?" I asked.

"I'm taking her back to her daddy," he replied. "Let him watch her bump into walls for a while."

I expected the shadow man to be standing there at the attic door when Alfie went through, but the room was as barren as the last time I had been up there. Not a soul in a soulless room. Alfie gave a shudder and a gasp as he looked around the place. He flung Flora around and into the center and then left.

"That's that," he said. Then he grabbed me and planted a big kiss right on my lips.

"Jesus, Alfie," I said, all flustered and taken aback. "I ain't never been kissed like that, not even in my life."

"I guess I'm hungry," he said. And then the big-dicked bastard did it again.

As we was coming down the stairs, we heard a commotion. The only thing I could think of was that Jimmy had fallen while making his way to the bathroom. But the grays were moaning something awful, like they was scared. I raced down the steps and indeed Jimmy's bed was empty, the sheets twisted onto the floor. The grays were standing about carping and staring down the hallway to the bathroom.

I let the expletives fly when I saw what they were looking at. The shadow man wasn't in the attic because he was down here, and he was attacking Jimmy in the hallway. The glamour still worked a bit, but it was wearing off. The shadow man was pushing Jimmy this way and that, circling him like a dark cyclone. I don't know what Jimmy thought was happening. Maybe he thought he had a touch of vertigo, because he just sat down against the wall and covered his head.

"Stop!" I screamed, furious at the shadow man, not really expecting him to pay me any mind.

But he did.

"Aw, fuck," Alfie muttered.

The shadow man pulled himself up to his full height, showed his ugly twisty-turny face, and roared most fiercely. I wasn't about to run, so I roared back. To my surprise, Alfie took up a roar as well. And even a few of the grays who hadn't fled into the walls, well, their moans began to change into groans. The shadow man at once hissed and flew straight up through the floorboards to the attic where his daughter Flora waited for him.

Alfie was smiling when I turned to face him. "Holy shit," he said with a relieved laugh. "We just scared the shadow man."

"At least for a bit," I said as Jimmy, recovering from his vertigo, got to his feet and walked past us and climbed back into bed. "Nessa needs to strengthen Jimmy's glamour, though. And I need to get him out of here and back to Leroy."

* * * *

Bull was snarling at me on his leash when I returned to seek Nessa's help. He was formless, just a black mass tied to a stick and slobbering anger and hate. But his growl had a dark echo to it that put the chills in me. It was like a great rusty barn door opening and exposing some hidden evil.

Nessa sat in her rocking chair on the porch with Dog right there beside her. He sensed my presence, I was certain. His ears peaked, and he let loose a solitary whine.

"Hush now, Ray," Nessa said to the dog. "He ain't gonna hurt ya. He wants to talk, is all." She stood and stretched like someone who's had a good night's sleep, a sleep devoid of nightmares. "Come on in," she said to me. "We'll talk inside."

I was surprised to be invited inside the shack. The glamour was gone, but still, I dared not go in without being asked first. I followed her, but Dog stayed on the porch. I kept my eyes on him. I still held some resentment towards him like he most likely still held the taste of me in his mouth.

The first thing I noted about being inside of Nessa's shack is that it sure didn't match the outside. In fact, it wasn't her shack I had entered at all, but her mind. There I was again in that beautiful inner land of pillars, waterfalls, soft breezes, and blue skies that went on forever. Nessa, the younger version of the woman I knew, turned around as she led me to the overview of the falls, and she smiled.

"There you are," she said. "You becomin' the man I recognize now. Got some meat on your bones."

I looked at my hands, and sure enough, I was no longer the walking skeleton I had been last time I was here. I had flesh, though still gaunt.

"You'll be pretty in no time," she said, leaning over the rock wall to look down at the falls. I stood beside her. "What you need, pretty boy? What you come to me for?"

"I need a new glamour," I said, "for Jimmy. The shadow man is harassing him again."

She hummed something soft and sweet. Her inner voices chimed in like a chorus. I might have thought it pretty if I hadn't been waiting on a reply.

"Can you help him, Miss Nessa?" I asked. "Can you give him a new glamour?"

"No." It was a blunt answer and one I was not expecting to hear.

"No?"

"No, Charlie." She turned to look at me. "You doin' good with your possessions. I saw the way you got into that Bull. You doin' real good. Without you, I'da never been able to take my revenge on him. I sleep sweetly now, and that's due to you. You just keep workin' at it. You soon be strong enough to take Jimmy's body on a trip. He needs to get to Leroy. No more glamours."

I admit to being a little irritated by this. "But what if the shadow man attacks again?" I protested. "I can't protect Jimmy against that darkness. Why won't you help me, goddammit?"

"I didn't say I wasn't gonna help ya, Charlie boy. Did you hear me say that? Because I did not say that. Now you just calm yourself down. I said I wasn't gonna put no glamour on him. You need to think before you speak at me with that tone of voice. Now you best apologize." Her inner voices took up the call as well. I felt like I was in the middle of church being renounced a sinner.

"I'm sorry, Miss Nessa."

"Alright, then," she said. "I've been readin' through my momma's books, and I came across somethin' that might just get rid of your shadow man for good. It involves the other spirits in the house, the sad lonely ones I feel every time I go in there."

"The grays?"

"There's only one problem. I need to find where this shadow man hid their bodies after he was through with them. You know, when he was the caretaker. There's most likely a mass grave somewhere. It should be close by too."

I must have been smiling something crazy, because she looked at me like she wanted me right out of her head. "What's wrong with you, boy?" she said. "You are disturbin' me with that grin."

"I know where they are, Miss Nessa," I answered. "I know where every last one of them bodies is."

I followed her to the carnival. Dog also followed at a loyal distance. Nessa knew where the haunted house was located from her childhood there. Before I left her head, I explained to her, too, that if she planned to exhume any bodies, my friend Alfie's was in the fun house.

The carnival spirits came out of the woods and the woodwork as she walked about the place searching for something to wheel all the pieces of Alfie's mutilated body from the fun house to the haunted house. She found an old, half-rotted dolly leaning against the cannibal man's cage. I had no idea what her intentions were, and a confused commotion erupted from the spirits as well. *What was she doing?* they wondered. *Why was she wheeling Alfie's remains into the haunted house? And without Alfie there to say yay or nay about it?*

Nessa had a straight face through the whole ordeal. She must have been disgusted at the sight of Alfie, and then disgusted even more by the "mannequins" in the haunted house, but she never let it show. And I knew she felt the plurality of spirits thick around her, as did Dog, but to their credit, neither of them so much as shook or whimpered.

The carnival spirits followed us into the haunted house, where Nessa wheeled the dolly with Alfie's remains into the center of the front parlor. I was expecting some big ceremony. Some magic words that would give me the shivers, maybe even send me running. But there was nothing. Nessa simply knocked over a can of petrol she had carried in her backpack, lit a big ol' match, and whoosh! The floor surrounding Alfie went up in flames. Nessa and Dog were out of the haunted house in a blink, but I stayed inside, as did all the carnival spirits. I didn't understand what good burning the place down would do at first, but then, as the bodies began to catch fire and cremate, as smiles of epiphany began to form on the carnival spirits' faces, I got it. Nessa was setting them free. Soon the whole place was ablaze, and there I remained, watching it like I was in the middle of some dazzling light show on the Fourth of July. Alfie's glass casing finally broke because of the heat, the green goo spilling to the floor, and at last he started to burn. Furniture was consumed and walls crawled with flames. And one by one, the carnival spirits closed their eyes, grinned authentic grins, and were borne away, like they was in some Rapture. Fuck me, it was something to see.

Nessa was gone from the carnival by the time I got back outside, the haunted house a funeral pyre behind me, so I went on back to the caretaker's house. Alfie came running towards me before I even stepped a foot on the porch, a changed man. There was a spring in his step, and he wore a smile as big as a slice of the biggest juiciest summer watermelon.

"Somethin's happened," he said excitedly. "I don't know what, but...oh boy! Can you feel it? Things are happenin' now, Charlie boy."

"What do you mean?" His grin was infectious.

He took my hand and pulled me towards the house. "The grays are fully awake," he said, "and they're pissed. Come see for yourself."

True enough, inside the house the grays were a crowd of anger. Yet on their faces was some kind of delight as well, as if they had made a decision and it had been unanimous. Me and Alfie stood back and watched as the grays assembled at the bottom of the stairs and slowly began to climb it as a group. The steps creaked and moaned like I never heard before as they ascended like they was on an escalator or something. Alfie and me followed.

They flowed through the attic wall like a flood of clay, and there was the shadow man, making a meal out of his daughter once again. She was on her hands and knees, trembling and choking as the black mass covered her and slid down her throat. The grays did not pause to take the sight in, nor did they seem at all frightened or concerned. Cal was the first to reach out and grab a wisp of shadow. The shadow man let go his hold on Flora and bellowed at Cal, but by that time, the former animal tamer had grabbed a substantial amount of darkness in his hands and was rending it away, twisting and tearing it. Others joined in, ripping at the shadow man with a dark glee as a horrid screeching filled the house. The shadow man tried to get away, to free himself from the ripping and the tearing, from the biting and the consuming, but there was no having it. The grays were frenetic, and even Flora finally joined in, crawling towards her daddy and stuffing a large piece of shade in her mouth. Scraps of shadow flew this way and that. Wherever they landed, they were stomped on or picked up and eaten. I did see one sliver, one tiny fragment of shadow, sink into the floor before it could be gotten to, but that was it. When the grays had finished, the shadow man was no more, and they walked right past me and Alfie with truly satisfied faces. The attic at once felt lighter, less heavy. We followed the grays down the steps—Cal, Flora, all of them—and watched them from the parlor's bay window as they walked into the sun and then fanned out and disappeared into the woods.

"Well, how ya like that?" said Alfie. "How the hell do ya like that?"

* * * *

The house was quiet after that. By quiet, I mean there was no more fear of the shadow man blocking up the hallways; the grays had vanished. Not one of them came back after disappearing into the woods. I didn't know what had happened to them. I thought maybe they'd found their ways to the Evermore, that happily ever after land I had seen when I first died. Then again, maybe they were just out wandering the woods.

Me and Alfie watched after Jimmy even as he started seeing to his own needs a little better. He was feeding and bathing himself now, and every so often, he'd try his hand at cleaning up. He was never much good at that, though. And fatigue was a daily battle.

I was becoming a master at possessing the bigger animals of the woods—a wolf here, a bobcat there. Once I even tried on the body of a big ol' stallion that had gotten loose from someone's farm. The fact that I wasn't tired at all after running for miles is what convinced me I'd be able to wear Jimmy soon. Still, the thought of my wearing Jimmy felt weird. It just didn't sit right with me. I mean, I knew it was for his own good, but… I guess the point being, never get to know the people you possess. Someone should write that in a handbook for the deceased.

One night as me and Alfie was playing a game of "which wall am I hiding in," Alfie said, quite out of the blue, "I wonder what happened to my strongman." I realized then that this was something that had been on his mind for some time, probably long before I was even born, because he was murdered years before that. It must have been torture for him. Well, I knew what I had to do. It was just gonna break my heart to get it done.

"Let's go into Devlin," I told him the next morning.

He shrugged and said, "Okay."

We walked and talked about silly things. We goofed off and met a few lost souls along the way, some of them kind, others suspicious. I suppose he just thought it was a nice day out, and it was, truly. But it had purpose.

Carter's apartment had yet to be rented out. Not too many folk were keen to rent a place where someone had died in such a grotesque manner, I guess. And honestly, it still smelt a bit. His body had probably been lying there for a week before being found. The human body requires way too much upkeep. You let it sit for too long, and it'll spoil.

"Do ya know someone who lives here, Charlie boy?" Alfie asked as we made our way into the building.

"Kinda," I said. "But I think you may know him better."

He looked at me all queer-like, and then we pushed through the walls to see Carter the violinist, Carter the strongman, not as I had known him, balding and pockmarked by grief, but as he was in his younger years—a large muscular man with a full head of hair and a smooth face. He was sitting naked on the floor, legs crossed, when he saw us. His eyes were on me first, and he rose, his big body taking on a defensive position.

"Death," he said. "Have you come for me, Death? Am I gonna have to pay for—"

Then he saw Alfie, and at once his whole body changed. He relaxed, as if melting.

Alfie looked at me, then back to Carter. No questions were asked. Nothing more was said, really. Just some choked attempts at apologies and love as they embraced one another. Lost souls found. At last.

I left Alfie there and walked back home. He was where he was meant to be all along. That was what would bring him his peace. I wiped a tear from my eye. Sure, I was happy for him. He was a good fella, my friend Alfie. But he was my friend Alfie. And I didn't expect to see him ever again.

Without Alfie, without even the grays to amuse me, I found the days at Jimmy's place very boring. I was becoming that storied old ghost that haunts a house. I did enter Jimmy's head more and more as the days went by. The hallways of his soul were ever-changing, so I never got bored there. Everything was in a constant state of construction, demolition, or reconstruction, and the hollow sound of heart against bone echoed through it all. His voices were, for the most part, quiet now. I knew what that meant. He was very close to accepting that he would never see Leroy again. That was bullshit.

One night while searching his head, walking it like it was some big archaeological site, I quite unexpectedly found a door. It was just an ordinary wood door with a brass handle, but the fact that it was there in his head at all was what made it such a thing. There were no doors in Jimmy's head, just archways. Hesitantly, I knocked. There was no answer, so of course, I entered without knocking a second time.

Immediately, I heard a crowd of voices—not Jimmy's, mind you—rush around me in excitement. They were shouting and whispering my name—it was Leroy's voice. Running towards me, down a long narrow cave, was a rather large person with arms outstretched. I was so taken aback by the sight of the figure that I was tempted to reach for the door and quickly make my way out. However, upon seeing Leroy's smiling face, I stayed. He picked me up and swung me around.

"Charlie boy!" he hollered. "What are you doin' here? Here in my very own dreams?"

"This is your head?" I asked after he put me down. "I was just walking through Jimmy's mind and I found that door. What the hell is going on?"

Leroy looked healthy and strong here. I wondered if it was a mirror of how he looked in real life now.

"That damn door," Leroy spat out. "I try to go through it every night, tryin' to talk to Jimmy. Some nights I can get through, but the damn fool won't even notice me. It's like I'm a ghost in his thick head."

"He thinks you left him, Leroy. He thinks you done split on him, that you wasn't happy."

His face was horrified, and his hands went to his hips. "That piece of chicken shit! What got that notion in his head?"

I told him all about Bull beating the shit out of Jimmy, about Leroy's brother and sister taking him while Jimmy was incapacitated, and about all the other shit we been through. You never seen a ghost look more wrecked than Leroy after that. He slid down against the wall of the cave with his hands to his head.

"That's why he hasn't come for me," he said in a voice of true comprehension. "Why would… He knows I'll die without him. I know that sounds cheesy, Charlie boy. I know it does. But it's true. I will die without him."

"Why don't you come on back to the house?" I asked, kneeling down beside him. "The grays are all gone."

"I cain't. I'm still pretty sick. I'm up and walkin' now, but nowhere good enough to head out on my own. And my family is watchin' me like I got the family jewels. My brother most of all. Ernie's a right piece of shit." He grabbed my hand. "Charlie boy, you gotta convince Jimmy to come get me. At least convince him to see me in his dreams on the nights I can get through that door."

"I've been trying to do just that, Leroy. Jimmy won't hear it, though."

"That thick-headed bastard." A smile flashed across his face. "Charlie," he said, serious as a stroke. "A person doesn't need to die to become a ghost."

I gave Leroy a big hug, and then I went back into Jimmy's head, trying to find him, to tell him what Leroy had just said. I knew it was true, too, the thing about not needing to die to be a ghost. I had seen Patricia after all, and if there was more proof for a living ghost on the planet, well, I didn't need it.

I couldn't find Jimmy, though, and after a bit, I gave up the search. Sometimes Jimmy just didn't want to be found. Sometimes he went so deep into himself I wondered if he was ever gonna find his way out again. People…they think too much, and most of it is bad shit.

Nessa visited the house the next day like a vision of augury. Jimmy was sitting on the porch swing, the first time he'd done that since Leroy'd been taken. I saw it as progress. He watched Nessa approach with her burlap sack, but said nothing. Seeing that she wasn't gonna get an invitation, she came up on the porch anyway and sat down right beside him.

"It's good to see you finally up and about," she said. "A body needs motion. A body craves motion."

He said nothing, didn't even look at her.

"Not talkin', huh? Well, that's fine. You just sit there and you listen to me, Jimmy. You listen good and hard. I know what you thinkin'. Yes, I do. You thinkin' about throwin' it all away. You thinkin' of forgettin' all about this life you had here with Leroy. Tryin' to forget it all. Maybe even burnin' the house down. But there ain't no reason for that nonsense, ya hear me? Them was good times you had with Leroy. You cain't burn memories away. And without Leroy…you'd never survive. I see the way ya flinch every time I say his name." She paused and stared him down. "Dammit. I'll say it again. Leroy, Leroy, Leroy! I'll say it all day if I have to, because ya gotta remember that you alive. You still alive, ya damn fool! You and I both know Leroy didn't leave ya. You the only two what can stand to be around each other. No. He out there waitin' for ya so ya best get some strength and get your ass ready for a trip, because you gonna take one. You gonna go find Leroy, ain't that right, Charlie boy?"

I couldn't help but give a loud "Yeah" even if it went unheard. Nessa was giving Jimmy that kick in the balls he needed. I just had to figure out how this great journey was gonna happen.

Jimmy looked at Nessa with a grief-stricken and questioning expression.

"I know, baby," she said. "But ya just gotta be ready to go, is all. I know ya sick, ya tired, ya don't wanna do nothin' because ya so damn sad. That's why ya got me, and that's why ya got Charlie. We gonna take the trip with ya, both of us, because, just like you, we got to move on too."

* * * *

I finally came up with a plan on how to get Jimmy to Leroy that didn't involve me taking over poor Jimmy's body. Now, it was a crazy plan, sure, like something straight out of a fantasy book. But after being dead for months now and seeing the things I had seen, I knew anything was possible. Anything anyone can think of, in fact. There was a lot of head hopping going on, and you can take that literal. Between Nessa and Jimmy, I didn't know where I was gonna spend my day. Leroy had told me he was at his family's home, so I hopped in on Jimmy to get directions. Couldn't find him at first, so I hopped on over to Nessa to tell her of my plan. When she couldn't get the directions from Jimmy either, I hopped back in on Jimmy, intent on getting what I came for, even if I had to wrestle it from him. I finally found him way back in a secluded dark room. His whispering voices told me the way over his refusal. Then I went back to Nessa to give her the directions. My lord, I was wore out by the end of it, and I hadn't even possessed no one.

The night we were set to go—and we chose night because, well, it would make our travel a bit less conspicuous—Alfie showed up at the front door as polite as a boy on his first date. Never expecting to ever see him again, I was immediately concerned. He had found his strongman, Carter, and his killer had been silenced as well. Why wasn't he in the Evermore?

The look on his face was one of muddled apprehension. He looked at me, at the porch, back at me, at the yard behind him, then back to me again.

Slowly, a grin crept over his face, and he pointed a finger at me in acknowledgement. "I know you," he said. "I know that face. You're Charlie."

"Yessir," I said. "Hey there, Alfie. It's good to see you again. But what are you doing here? Where's Carter?" I looked for him, but he was nowhere about.

Again, that confused look shrouded Alfie's features as he mumbled Carter's name to himself like he was trying to remember who the strongman was. His eyes lit up at last. "Carter. Yeah. My strongman. He went on ahead. Just faded into the Evermore. You shoulda seen it, Charlie."

"Without you? But you was supposed to go with him, Alfie."

"Oh, don't you worry none, Charlie boy." He put a hand on my shoulder. "I told him I'm followin' real soon. But there was somethin' I needed to do first."

"What's that, Alfie?"

"What?" He cocked his head.

"What was it that you had to do first?"

There was a moment's pause. It seemed as if it was taking all his strength just to try and remember me. Or rather, to not forget me.

"I remember you," he said again with a sweet smile. "You're Charlie. I just came by, Charlie, I just came by to say…goodbye. I just wanted to tell you goodbye and that I was movin' on now. Goin' to the Evermore. You been a friend to me."

If I had a heart, it was breaking.

"And I wanted to say too…I wanted to…to tell you, thank you. Thank you for showin' up at the carnival and for burnin' the place down"—he chuckled here, and his eyes got all glassy and watered up—"and for showin' me I still had power after all. And for Carter. Thank you for bringin' him on back to me, Charlie. For that most of all, I think."

I couldn't control myself any longer. I leaned in and gave him a big hug. "I'm gonna miss you so much, Alfie," I sobbed.

"Ah, c'mon now," he said, patting me on the back.

When we pulled back from each other, I saw he was crying too. Then he wiped the tears and looked at his hands like he hadn't ever seen wet before.

"You're the best friend I ever had," I said.

He grinned. "You're the only friend I ever had, Charlie boy."

He turned and started walking away. "You know," he said as he went, "there are still some grays and carnival spirits around, hangin' out in the woods and such. They'll help you if you need 'em. They owe ya." Then he stopped, raised his head, and sniffed the air like he smelt something delicious. He looked at me, eyes still wet with tears, and he said, "See ya in the Evermore, Charlie boy."

And then my friend Alfie disappeared.

* * * *

"You here, Jimmy?" I called out as I walked the halls of Jimmy's head. "Now you call out to me if you're here. I ain't got time for games."

There was no response other than the inner voices whispering things that might make sense individually, but when spoken in unison were like thousands of vines climbing up the same tree. It was dark in this area of his psyche. On the outside, he seemed to be progressing, waking up, but you couldn't tell it from inside his head.

Tired of searching, I stood still. "Well, we're heading on out, Jimmy. We're gonna go find Leroy. We're gonna get the two of you back together, and I don't need to possess you to do it."

The whispers hushed in a gasp so quickly that I heard my own voice echo through Jimmy's head.

"You think it'll work?" Jimmy, the young Jimmy I knew, formed out of the dark like he had been there the whole time. "Do ya think Leroy will be waitin' for me?" His eyes were filled with hope and doubt.

"I know he will, Jimmy. He told me so."

Jimmy sighed. "I hope you're right, Charlie boy. I do."

"I am. You'll see. You just gotta do what Nessa tells you to do, you hear?" I looked around the dim halls that surrounded us. "And Jesus Christ, Jimmy. Would it hurt to redecorate this place?"

* * * *

I was out on the porch with Jimmy when Nessa came walking down the drive. She had her spear in hand and carried her burlap sack over her shoulder stuffed with god knows what. At her side walked Dog. Jimmy remained seated in the porch swing, but I went to meet her. She searched the ground for my family of spiders.

"Evenin', Charlie boy," she said as she kept on walking. "We ready to do this?"

I wasn't sure. Honestly, this was gonna be a big undertaking. I don't even think she was certain we could pull it off. But we had to try.

She sat beside Jimmy on the swing, Dog at her feet. "The journey's upon us," she said to him. "I know you well rested, that's for sure. You ain't done nothin' but rest lately. So it's time to wake up now, ya hear me? Imma drive the Buick. You can either ride with me or stay here in the house. It's your choice."

He shook his head and looked off to the side with his arms now folded across his chest.

"Fine, then. You can stay here. That'll save me from doin' any unnecessary chattin'."

It was a joke that Jimmy didn't seem to appreciate.

"There'll be five of us in all on this little excursion," she said. "I imagine it'll be quiet for the most part from here on out. You ain't talkin' much. Me, I only speak when things need sayin', and Ray here only barks when warnin'. Charlie boy's silent to us all and, bless him, don't take up no room. And Bull"—she reached into her burlap sack and brought out a mason jar clouded and crowded with darkness, like rotting peaches—"Bull ain't gonna be causin' no one any problems at all." She said it with a note of pride and victory as she inspected the jar for probably the millionth time. I don't blame her.

* * * *

A bit earlier that day, I took Alfie's advice and sought out the help of the grays. To be honest, I didn't see my plan working at all without their help, though I didn't tell Nessa that. I wasn't absolutely certain she'd come with if she knew the grays would be making the trip as well. But heck, maybe she knew all along. She was a witch, after all. Maybe she was psychic too.

I walked out into the woods just as the sun was starting its descent in the western sky. The light was breaking through the tree branches and the leaves, but not enough to say the forest was well-lit. I had no real idea where to begin looking for the grays, so I just stood in the middle of the woods and shouted like an idiot. I said, "Is anybody there? Do you remember me? It's… It's Charlie. Charlie from the house, the house that used to belong to the caretaker. Alfie said you might want to help me. If that's so," I said as I turned in a full circle, "I would surely appreciate it."

There was no answer for a few minutes, just the sound of the birds overhead and a light breeze brushing through the leaves and carrying elementals on past me. I was readying myself to leave, to give up and go back to the house where I could try and think of some other way to get Jimmy to Leroy, but then I saw a face. It appeared slowly, like when you think you see a shape in the clouds, but you know it ain't real. Only this was real, and it got more real the longer I looked at it. This was a pale face, and it belonged to a tall man. This was Cal, and there was Flora forming right near him. Soon others formed until they were all around me, just appearing out of thin air, an army of pale-faced slender men and slender women too. They stood there, gaping at me with blank faces. I didn't know whether to back away slowly or run.

"I-I could really use your help, if you'd be so kind," I said with a bit more respect. "I need some help…with that ol' house, you see. I can't do it alone. Ain't got the strength."

No sound, no movement. Just dead faces, emotionless, taut, blank. I stood there for an awkward moment more before I made my exit. If they were going to help me, I assumed they would follow me out of the woods, so I turned around and began marching. Only they didn't follow. Over my shoulder, I saw they were still standing there, just watching me, some of them blending back in with the trees or vanishing altogether.

I waited for a good hour when I got back to Jimmy's house. I sat on the porch steps, but I saw not even a hint of gray coming from the forest. That's when Nessa came with her dog and her burlap sack. I didn't know what I was gonna tell her. There had to be another way. There just had to be. That's when I decided I'd have to do it myself. I hadn't actually tried it, after all. How hard could moving an old house be? It was an inanimate object, not a living creature with a will and a mind. *This*, I tried to convince myself, *would be a slice of cake.*

But I was once again wrong. I didn't even know where to begin when possessing a house. The very fact that it had no mind was what made it most confusing. If a home has a soul, it's something completely foreign to me. Maybe a house's soul is an amalgam of everyone who has ever lived there, of its very history, and if that is so, it would be a near-impossible feat for me. I got into the walls anyway, into the front parlor's support beams, but all I succeeded in doing was giving the house a few more creaks and groans. I didn't want to tear the parlor from the house, so I gave up and went back outside where I sat with Nessa and Jimmy. I didn't want to say I was giving up, but that's what it felt like. I felt like a damn loser, so I sulked.

"Looks like you ain't goin' nowhere in this house," Nessa said. "We can take the Buick, all of us."

"Ain't goin' nowhere is right," Jimmy said. "Nowhere, no how. Best just leave the past in the past and let me get on with things." His voice was flat, emotionless.

Then Dog's ears perked right up, and Nessa gave a sharp westerly glance to the woods. I stood when I saw what was coming from the trees. There was not only the color gray, but carnival colors as well, bleeding from the forest. Some of them were slow-going, crawling along the earth, while others were taking larger, more determined steps.

"Who that be, Charlie?" Nessa asked, rising to her feet.

I wanted to laugh and jump and slap my thighs and say, "That be the grays and the carnival spirits, Nessa! They're coming to help just like Alfie said they would." But all I did was grin like a damned fool as they dissolved into the house around us.

Nessa must have figured things out soon enough, though, because she grabbed her bag and her and Dog headed for the Buick. I stayed put on the porch with Jimmy, who was completely unaware anything was going on. But that obliviousness did not last long. No sir. When the house started moaning something awful, Jimmy looked around him, trying to figure out where the heck all that ruckus was coming from. And it was one hell of a caterwaul. Wood was splintering and pipes were buckling. Rusty steel and metal that hadn't been moved in years screeched in surprise as the spirits touched them and cast them anew. Why, it was as if the ol' place was yawning itself awake. It was at last gonna get up and move and no longer just loom. Jimmy clung to the swing as it pitched wildly about, going backwards and hitting the house and then swinging forward so far I was certain the chains were gonna snap and send Jimmy flying.

Finally, it was as if I was a whole man taller. Nessa was standing beside the Buick with the door open. Her eyes seemed wide in disbelief. I looked over the edge of the porch and saw for myself what stunned her so. That house had legs. They might have been pipes and wood beams and rusted metal fittings once, but they were legs now. Jimmy crawled inside the house at that point, and I was glad for it. I didn't want him hurt just as we got underway. But we weren't moving. The house was standing as if on stilts, one side higher than the other. Nessa had gotten into the car and was waiting, Dog barking out the window behind her. It took me a minute to realize that I was the captain of this lopsided ship and my crew needed to be told where to go, what to do.

"Follow that car!" I shouted, not needing to keep my balance yet still placing my grip on the front banister.

Night had settled in around us. The Buick's taillights were a lantern. The house's first steps were anxious, like a newborn or someone learning to walk again. Nessa slowly led the way ahead of us. The strides became jerky but not unbearable. I imagined Jimmy was having quite a ride in his parlor bed.

And so, at last, there we were. Leaving the basement behind, we headed out into the night, a witch driving a Buick with a reformed dog, a Bull stuffed in a mason jar, a man who had given up on love, a house possessed by carnival spirits, and me, the captain. Some might even say a hero. I had never felt as alive, so I shouted.

I did, I shouted, "Yee-haw!" Because, well, it seemed only appropriate.

We traveled at night. Even on back roads and abandoned highways, a walking house might seem a bit suspicious if sighted by the right vagabond. During the day, the house rested in old cornfields or vacant lots, in places where maybe a home had once stood long ago, but all that was left now was a few blocks of foundation or a crumbling chimney.

Jimmy stayed inside the house in the beginning. Once he got over his initial sea sickness, he fixed the bed so it wouldn't move and watched from the parlor's bay window as the old world slowly passed by. At night, Nessa would come into the house with Dog, if for no other reason than to be out of the Buick. She always brought the mason jar inside with her and sat it where she could keep an eye on it. That was a bit unnerving, but I saw the point. God forbid if she lost it or the damn thing broke and Bull was set free. She and Jimmy didn't talk much at all. She'd make them some supper, they'd eat, and then she'd read from one of her momma's books that was packed into the burlap sack. Dog would curl up on the floor beneath her. Jimmy would sleep.

The grays and the carnival spirits would go off into the dawn, treading slowly through the surrounding fields like servants of the fading moon. It was a damn eerie thing to watch. They'd all be back, though, by the time dusk came around. I wondered why these spirits hadn't gone on to the Evermore when Nessa had burnt them free. I guess some ghosts just gotta haunt for a while.

* * * *

I only got into Jimmy's head once when we were starting our journey. Truthfully, it was a damn depressing place to be, even for a dead fella like me. But I found him easily enough this time. No longer was he hidden away in some dank corridor or tiny chamber in his head. He was standing right there at Leroy's door with a puzzled look on his handsome face.

"It's Leroy, Jimmy," I said. "Go on through. You'll see. He's waiting for you."

"I know it's Leroy, Charlie boy," he replied. "I ain't no fool." He said this with a bit of the sweet sarcasm I once knew in him. "I can feel him on the other side like a heartbeat." He reached out and touched the center of the door.

"My god, you are exasperating! So if you know it's him, why ain't you going through to see him?"

"Because I want to see the real thing. I don't want to have conversations with some dream man." He sighed. "Go on through if you want, Charlie. Nobody's stoppin' ya. But I'ma wait." And he faded into his mind's blackness.

Well, I did go on through to see Leroy, but it wasn't the cheerful reunion I had experienced the first time. Instead of hallway, there was a white room, and in the center of it was Leroy in a bed much like the one in the house parlor. He was looking at me, gesturing me forward.

"What's happening, Leroy?" I asked. "You don't look well."

"Hey there, Charlie boy," he said, his voice a rasping whisper. "I'm slipping."

"We're coming. Just you hold on. We'll be there."

"Best be quick," he said. "I don't know how much longer I can hang on."

But my lord. How does a fella ask a walking house to hurry it up?

* * * *

Jimmy began sitting on the porch in the mornings after the night's crawl was over. The lopsided walk of the house seemed to soothe him to sleep, and he was adapting a more normal sleeping schedule, though he still took the occasional nap. He never left the porch to wander around or to discover any of the surroundings that changed on a daily basis. That was for the best. He was still a bit stumbly and lethargic.

Nessa always sat out with him for a couple hours in the morning before she would take her rest. This was very thoughtful of her since she was most likely beat from driving all night. There was an understanding between them. They sat right alongside one another on the porch swing with not a word crowding the space. They seemed equal in their own personal losses and balanced each other out well.

One morning, after Nessa had gone upstairs to sleep and Jimmy was out on the porch with Dog watching a sudden rain storm pass through, we had a visitor. A lumpy man who looked middle-aged and hummed a curious melody came nosing his way up onto the porch right past Jimmy and into the house. He searched through the old place, interest flagging with each shuffle of a step.

Finally, exasperated and with a scowl complete with a protruding bottom lip, he put his hands on his hips and said quite vociferously, "This is the boringest damn walkin' house I've ever seen!"

He stood in the pose for a good few well-rounded seconds before saying, "Well? Ain't it?"

He was talking to me, expecting an answer. I wasn't even sure he had seen me. Some spirits don't.

"We're traveling," I said. "It don't need to be a carnival. The fact that it walks should be entertainment enough, don't you think?"

"I suppose," he grumbled. "I suppose." He started humming again, eyeing the place like he was looking to buy.

"If it's a carnival you're looking for," I continued, "there's one back that way, towards Devlin. At least, the remains of one. Don't suppose there are any spirits there now to keep it going. But that's where I came from."

"Did ya now?" the man said, a big ol' grin on his face as he drew closer to me. In life, I imagined he smelt of whiskey and TV dinners. He gave me the once-over. "Was ya murdered there?"

"I was killed in Devlin, yes. But not in the carnival."

"That's too bad," he said, sounding disturbingly disappointed. "Woulda made quite a story if you'd been murdered in a carnival. Yessir. Woulda been quite a tale to tell. Might have even gotten my respect."

"Were you murdered, sir?" I countered.

His prideful buffoonery all but deflated before me. "No." He began walking around the house, looking at the turned-over furniture and the painting of Flora that still hung crooked on the wall.

"I choked on my beef stew while I was watchin' my favorite TV program."

"That's too bad," I said. "You must have a lot of unfinished business, huh?"

"No, no, not really. I had a good life. Just an inglorious death. Everything was pretty much perfect while I lived and breathed, though. No regrets." The blush in his cheeks looked like a half-ripe tomato.

"None?"

"Well…there was one. But it only happened because I choked"—he raised his voice in anger—"on that damn piece of beef!"

"I don't understand."

He drew closer to me again. "The TV show I was watchin', my favorite, was about a murder in a sleepy northern town. Nothin' on television like it. The entire run of the series was devoted to solving this one young girl's murder, you see. I loved it. Never missed it. Watched it religiously and I never did anything religiously, not even church. Well, because I choked to death before the mystery was solved, I never learned who killed that poor girl. It still makes me damn furious! I have to know who the killer was before I go on. I have to!"

Unbelievable, right? A TV show was that man's unfinished business. The fact was, from all my reading, I knew the answer he was looking for. I hadn't been born yet when that show was on, but I had found a stack of old magazines in the Devlin library dumpster after a renovation. One of these magazines happened to have an article discussing the whole series like it was real life or something. I didn't see any reason to keep that to myself if it'd help that absurd man move on to the Evermore, so I told him.

"That's the most ridiculous ending…" His eyes got as big as billiard balls. "I can't believe it! Are you certain?" He was incredulous, going around the room, kicking at furniture and swearing to high heaven. The commotion even woke Nessa up, who stood at the top of the stairs and looked down on our nothingness as a chair slid across the room or a book took to flight. He shouted a bunch more expletives, accused me of something incoherent, and then ran out of the house, cussing, ranting, and raving. And all I could think was *What a damn fool reason to still be here.*

He wasn't the only fool we had to deal with on our journey, either. I had noticed a while back a group of five teenagers following us. They were a few years younger than me and up to no good. What I mean by that isn't that they were wanting to cause harm to anyone or anything, but simply that their intent just wasn't productive. It was no good. Doesn't necessarily mean it was any bad, though. I walked over to their camp one morning and had myself a listen. They were brimming with ideas about how to get into the house, wondering what was powering it, who was driving the Buick. I don't think the fact that the house was honest-to-god possessed ever entered their heads. If it did, none spoke it, probably for fear of being laughed at by their friends.

They kept a good field's distance during the day and only crept along after our macabre parade at night with their headlights off. Being kids, and not terribly intelligent ones at that, their stealth went mute soon, and both Jimmy and Nessa realized we were being tailed. I could tell my two flesh-and-bone housemates were coming up with a bit of mischief without them even saying so. When the day arrived, when those kids finally snuck into the house, I just sat back on Jimmy's bed with my hands behind my head and watched the show.

Thinking the house was abandoned, seeing no sign of Jimmy, Nessa, or Dog, all five of the little ne'er-do-wells crept inside like the broad daylight cast no shadows. Jimmy was hiding for the time being, and that tickled me to no end, because I couldn't remember the last time I saw Jimmy as playful. Nessa was watching from the top of the stairwell with Dog. I wondered if she had given herself a glamour so the kids couldn't see her. I mean, she was right there if they had chanced to look up. Dog must have been in on the fun as well, because there wasn't even a loud pant from him.

One of the girls said, "Damn, ain't this weird? Just looks like a regular old house. I had an uncle who lived in a house like this. What you think powers it?"

"Prolly got a secret motor somewhere," said the leader, a freckle-faced redhead in a scarred leather jacket. "Maybe in the basement."

"It ain't got no basement," said another boy. "Just legs."

"Shut up," hushed the leader. They still hadn't managed to go farther than the parlor.

"This ain't right," said another boy in a more solemn tone. "Feels like a funeral home to me. Maybe we should get out of here. This place is…off."

"You're off," said the leader. "If you wanna go, then git. That just means more fame and glory for us when we bring this house to the world's attention. Ain't every day you see a walkin' house."

"We gonna steal it?" asked the other girl. "I don't want to be labeled a thief."

"How can you steal somethin' that ain't got no people in it?" the redhead asked. "Those folk we saw, the man on the porch and the woman in the car, clearly they lost control of their machine. It's done run off without 'em, see? And we found it."

"Or maybe," said the first girl, her voice shaking a bit.

"Maybe what?"

"Maybe they was ghosts." She froze in her tracks, as did a couple of the others. "Maybe this house is haunted."

Bingo.

"Balderdash!" said the leader. "Ain't no such thing as…"

But he never finished that statement because out of the small bathroom beneath the stairs came a low grumble. All heads turned that way. The grumble grew in size and strength until it was a roar. By this point, two of the kids was already gone, having split so fast their piss barely hit the floor.

The three that stayed, including the redheaded leader, were in for the real show, however, as Jimmy jumped out of the bathroom in no more than his socks and screamed, "I be Jehovah, the god of Sex, and I'ma rip your asshole apart!"

Well, that brought forth shrieks of terror from the remaining hoodlums. Two of them ran, but the redhead was so petrified he fell backwards, yelling holy hells and eyes wide with terror as Jimmy walked towards him in an affected manner. The boy was still screaming as Jimmy dragged him out the front door.

"You're lucky," Jimmy snarled. "I don't like ginger boys." He threw the boy off the porch and watched, laughing full-bellied, as the poor kid, at last finding his legs, soon outran his fellow snoopers.

The ol' house was filled with laughter for the first time since Leroy had left. Jimmy was laughing at what he had just done, Nessa was laughing at Jimmy, and me…I was laughing because it felt so damn good. For once, the tears in this house were silver, not black.

* * * *

As I walked out one morning after the house had come to a rest, I came across someone I did not expect. The fog was as thick as soup and the grays were quickly consumed by it. The carnival spirits, though brighter, were soon gone from my sight as well, until it seemed I was alone in the world. The field before me was revealed one step at a time until I came upon the silhouette of a hill and atop that hill a small willowy dancing tree. But then I heard the sound of others approaching, the sound of chains and dragging feet. I thought at first it might be a farmer, but the season for farming was over. Through the fog the shadowed figure of a woman appeared on the hill, and in her hand, she held what seemed a leash. Coming behind her and attached to the leash were a group of seven men. As she approached I recognized the black gown and the long blonde hair as that of Patricia. She was younger, but it was no doubt her. Of the young men in her wake, all beautiful and bound at the neck, I only knew Orlando. Exactly when they had all died, I couldn't tell. But Patricia looked resolved and at least content to be dead. I guess the ability to move around on her own again had stirred in her some sort of determination. I would have even said she was happy if not for the blackness in her eyes.

She hardly noticed me, but her beautiful leashed things stared at me for help, especially Orlando.

"Patricia," I said. "When did you die?"

The simple question made her glance at me with her familiar expression of contempt. "After you, my boy," she said, and without a note of apology, she continued. "After Carter killed you."

I walked along with her, far enough away to avoid the stench of apathy that clung to her like perfume. "But why is Orlando dead? And who are all these other fellas?"

"You're such a nosy, troublesome boy," she said, not even bothering to look at me as she led her pack. "I killed myself, Charlie. Shot myself in the head. The blood blossomed on the wall like a gorgeous rose. I had Orlando bound to me before that with a spell and killed him as well. Arsenic, the same manner in which I killed all my pretty things before him. Pretty things are often stupid and very easy to trick. There was a funny thing to Orlando's death, though. When he died, his Death was not me but you." She looked at me accusingly. "I wonder why that is. My other pretty things had been stumbling around the house for years. They were all quite easy to catch."

Orlando's eyes were sad and pleading as he stared at me. He was going gray. But I had no idea how to undo Patricia's spell. He tried to pull away once, to get out of his chains, but Patricia jerked him back into submission.

"Where are you going, Patricia?" I asked.

"My ex-lover died, the one who was the cause of my misery." She grinned like a hungry cat. "I'm off to pay my respects. I'm off to collect."

She paused and stood completely still, then turned slowly around and said to me, with an eyebrow raised, "Would you like to come along? You're very pretty, Charlie. You'd make a nice addition to my charm bracelet here."

I backed away. "No, thank you, ma'am."

She stared a moment longer. I knew what was going through her head.

"Don't worry, Charlie," she said. "I'm not going to take you. Not yet. Be on your way, and I'll be on mine, you bothersome boy. Maybe I'll come back for a visit someday. You still reside in Devlin, don't you?"

And with that same cat-like grin, she turned back around and vanished into the fog, leading her beautiful things over the hills. Orlando gave me one last plea before his face was shrouded by gray mist. That woman was a spider. Orlando was a fly.

* * * *

We rested the house for what would turn out to be the final time on a hill that overlooked a large valley. But this wasn't no ordinary valley. That's to say, the valley itself was plain enough, but it was filled with ghosts of giants. At least, that's what it seemed at first. Some conceptual artist, most likely from one of them big cities, had erected what Jimmy called an installation that covered the entire field below the hill. In the early morning hours, when the sun was just beginning to rise and the mist had yet to clear, that valley looked more haunting than any spirit I'd yet to see. There were hundreds of faceless white balloon men with their arms to the heavens, the kind you see at a car dealership, waving and dancing in the breeze. Only it wasn't breezy. On closer inspection, I saw there was a loud fan below each one, keeping it dancing with the others. I don't know art, and neither, it seemed to me, did this artist.

As I walked between the dancing men, I would every so often catch a quick glimpse of other spirits—some of them the grays from the house, others completely foreign to me—staring up at the installation or looking out at me. They were visible to me for no more than a snap of the fingers, and then they were out of my sight again, curtained by a courteous bow from a dancing man before vanishing altogether. I hated seeing spirits that way. Quick flashes of dead eyes made clear their intent: they wanted me to know they were there. The dead are always watching. You know when you're naked in the bath and the thought passes through your head that, *Hey, I wonder if there are ghosts here in this room watching me bathe?* Or you're in bed at night shooting your wad and for the tiniest of seconds you think, *I wonder if I'm entertaining some spirit.* Well, don't fool yourself by shrugging it off. You are.

As the morning came up, the valley looked more inviting. I traveled down the hill once again, this time with Nessa, Dog, and Jimmy. It took me by surprise, but Jimmy decided to finally leave the confines of the house. We walked slowly between row upon row of dancing men, watching as they performed their pointless ballet in the morning sun, their arms and bodies bending and kowtowing to some silent gorgeous music. It was a wonderful morning, the warmth of the sun and the warmth of friendship combined. I think I realized then that there is a line of beauty to every twisted thing, a perfection to everything that's broken. A thing can only flow when it's in motion, after all, and to be in motion, a thing has to break its perfect stance, its perfect stillness. Only broken things are perfect things.

"They look like they're wavin' goodbye," said Jimmy as he stood staring up with his arms folded.

"Maybe," said Nessa, standing beside him. "Or maybe they givin' thanks. Maybe there be a god they all dancin' for."

"Goodyear?" joked Jimmy. He was still getting his bearings, fighting the urge to become an agoraphobe.

"You laugh, baby," she said with a smile. "But everything has a spirit."

"Even tall arm-wavey things from car lots?"

"Everything comes from somethin'," she replied with a shrug. "Everything got some form of energy wrapped up inside it, and energy don't die. It finds a way to exist, no matter."

"So, you and me, we're gonna live forever?"

"Yessir," she said. "We are like gods, you and me. We are like vessels holdin' godstuff."

He smiled. "I like that, Miss Nessa. That's some damn fine theology."

Dog had been barking and jumping up at the dancing men, finally wagging that tail for play. Jimmy ran off, frolicking with him, clapping his hands and whistling. I could see them through the dancing men: Jimmy laughing, Dog's tail springing back and forth like a crazy windshield wiper. *They should get a dog*, I thought. When Jimmy finds Leroy, they should settle down somewhere and get themselves a big ol' hound to play with.

"I done told your ghost friends they can leave," Nessa said to me once Jimmy had gone off to play. "I thanked 'em for their help. We're gonna stay here. We don't need 'em no more." She kept walking, slow and easy. She looked more relaxed than I'd ever seen her. Maybe that was because she did not have her burlap sack with her to weigh her down. She'd left it at the house.

"Leroy is right near here," she continued, "if those directions he gave you are correct. I'm gonna go find him today. You stay here with Jimmy. I'll try to be back tonight. Once Jimmy is back with Leroy, I can get on back home." She looked to the ground for my family of spiders. "And so can you, Charlie boy."

The Evermore. I had almost forgotten about it. Was I really that close? How could I forget about the Evermore?

Nessa and I left the dancing men in their field as Jimmy and Dog continued to play. Nessa was intent on leaving right soon. We had new adventures we were eager to begin. When we entered the house, however, I felt an immediate pang of darkness. Nessa felt it, too, so much so that she gasped for air. She ran into the kitchen. The look on her face as she stood over the spilt contents of her burlap sack told me all I needed to know. Books were scattered, papers mussed, and the jar holding Bull…it wasn't gone. No. It was shattered. And the glass that had been so cloudy and dark was now clear.

"The leash is broken now," she said, as heartbroken as if she was telling me her momma had died. "That sonbitch is free." She went to her knees and investigated the shards. "Mason jars don't break easy," she said. She closed her eyes. "He nowhere around the house. Not that I can feel."

She was right. Bull was nowhere to be seen, and if he was still in the house, there would be a filth starting to collect, a layer of shadow. Still, I was uneasy. I felt something, some spirit, in the house, and not of the grays or the carnival folk. That spirit wasn't wanting to be seen. I was watched. The ol' house groaned in agreement at my concern.

Nessa rose, grabbing her books and things and stuffing them haphazardly back into the burlap sack. "I'm gonna go find Leroy," she said. "When Bull comes back, I suspect he gonna be after me. Ain't no glamour gonna protect any of us. His anger done grown beastly if he can break free from one of my jars. Best to get myself far away from here so ya don't get caught up in the mix. You watch over Jimmy, Charlie boy. Keep him safe. I'll read through Momma's journals. There has to be a way to kill a demon." She paused and looked around the kitchen for a sign of me. "I'm truly sorry, Charlie boy. It was my own need for vengeance that kept Bull in that jar. I shoulda destroyed him outright. Now I've gone and fucked things up."

I watched from the porch as Jimmy and Dog continued to play among the dancing men down below. Nessa peeled out in the Buick, off to find Leroy. What she would see when she found Leroy was anyone's guess. Last I had seen him, he was slipping back into a coma. Maybe all my trying had been for naught. Bull was on the loose again, Leroy was slipping, and there was something new in the house with me. And it was still watching.

* * * *

Nessa still wasn't back by the time night had fallen, and with the grays and carnies gone from the house, it was just me, Jimmy, and Dog. Jimmy fell asleep fast enough, cuddled up with Dog in the bed. The house was desolate and dark without electricity, but the moon spilt some of her milk through the windows. I watched my friend sleeping for a bit, still anxious about what unseen thing was in there with us, and then I stepped out onto the porch. The dancing men continued their revelry or whatever it was, but now it seemed more menacing than in the daylight. Now it seemed they was looking up at the house, waiting for a sacrifice to be tossed down to them, a field of giant ghosts who were unstoppable in their zeal, who would rip the arms off a grown man if told to do so by their god.

The hinges of the porch swing creaked ever so slightly, yet it startled me. I looked to see Patricia sprawled out like a weeping Ophelia on the wicker. Her eyes were red, bright red, from weeping and her face ruddy from wiping. Her beautiful things—or something like them—surrounded her. There were seven figures, that much was for certain, but they were terrible to look upon. They were still in chains, yet Patricia no longer held them on a leash. They were no longer beautiful. They were charred husks of men, like dolls set on fire but not yet fully burnt. Their heads were like the pointy ends of wooden stakes, and their arms and legs were crisp and weed-like. I could not tell which was Orlando, and I wager neither could she. They cringed and lurched about with such agonizing steps around her it was painful just to watch them.

"Not so beautiful anymore, are they, Charlie?" she said, wiping her eyes as if it took all the strength she had.

"It was you, wasn't it?" I said. "It was you who broke the jar and freed Bull."

"Bull?" she said with a smile that was most likely meant to be condescending if she had had the energy to see it through. "Was that his name? Good grief. Yes, my dear Charlie. I set the Bull free from his pen."

"You crazy ol'… Why?"

"I've been watching you. I've been watching this house. Longer than you might think, actually. This witch friend of yours has some awesome powers. And a quiet rage. I respect that about her. She just needs to harness that energy."

"She's better than you, Patricia." I stayed where I was. I didn't want to be any closer than I was to that woman. "She'd see right through you if you ever tried anything, if you ever tried to possess her."

"Possess her?" She laughed. "I would never sully myself in someone else's flesh, especially someone as…" She flitted her hand as if she expected me to fill in the words myself. She sat rubbing her forehead. "I thought that if I could add this Bull to my collection, to my beautiful things, he could help me bring my ex to his knees. Oh, that would have been something to see! And it would have worked. When the jar broke, your Bull seemed just as confused as my beautiful things here. It was charming, really. Sure, he wasn't beautiful himself, but every family needs its charred black sheep. Don't you agree, Charlie?"

"So what happened?"

Her face bore an expression of disgust as she recounted. "Something, a small slither of blackness, a slice of shadow, an eye floater really, emerged from the floor and disappeared into him. Then he changed. His eyes suddenly became deeper, darker, more menacing. I wouldn't call it will, but there was definite power, desire. I ran. I hid. But my beautiful things, foolish boys, thinking he would free them, they all stayed, and he drank them up. Their screaming…

their screaming was…" She rubbed at her eyes again, this time furiously. "I closed my eyes and disappeared into these bug-infested walls. When I was sure he was gone, I came back to the kitchen and found my beautiful things, or what was left of them…"

"Do you love them, Patricia?" I asked. "Do you love them still?"

"What?" she growled, looking at me with eyes that could break promises in two.

"You told me once that love was a poison or something like that. But you seem to have drunk it right up, this poison. You just didn't know that's what it was. I guess it wasn't labeled properly for you. Your love for your ex caused you to seek love from others, from your beautiful things. And now that same poisonous love has destroyed everyone you've known. Think of how things might have been different if you'd just…moved on."

"Don't lecture me, you little whore," she hissed. "You know nothing of love. You sold yourself for money. I bought your love."

"No, Patricia. You bought my body. I never gave you love. Ever."

I left it at that, thinking we were through and she'd get the hell off the porch, and I went inside. But she followed me in her black gown just like the black husks of men followed her. Dog sensed her at once and woke Jimmy up with his barking.

"You don't walk away from me, boy. Not in life or death." She was furious, her face making an ugly show of itself. "Not in any life will you ever be better than me. You hear me?"

"Go back to Devlin," I said to her coolly. "Eek out a nonexistence there. I'm done with you here. I don't ever want to see you again. You were a sad old crone in life, and you're nothing but a waif of a spirit now. Why, I bet all the other spirits just sit back and laugh at you. You are pathetic, Patricia. Carter knew it. Orlando knew. I know it. You, though, you never knew much of anything."

She ran towards me, hands outstretched like pitchforks, as if she could ever harm me again. Dog was on the floor barking and growling and running in circles, and Jimmy knew something was amiss even if he couldn't see it. Things were becoming a little too agitated. Dog had encountered spirits more frightening than Patricia. I wondered why he was acting so crazy. And then I realized the truth of it. Dog wasn't carrying on about Patricia. There was something altogether more terrifying in the house now.

Patricia's fingers never reached me. Thick arms of black mist swirled about her, lifting her in the air, and she screamed. I couldn't tell if she was screaming for me to help her or not, the sound the great blackness made was such a clamor. I stared in shock for a moment as Orlando and the beautiful things were turned to dust in a second and Patricia began to crisp and blacken even as she screamed. The face that was drinking her was a distortion, a stretched and broadened fun-house version of Bull's face. The caretaker had returned.

I shouted for Dog and headed for the back kitchen door. Dog pulled at Jimmy's arm. Jimmy could not deny something was wrong. The house was shaking like it was being hit by a twister. He bolted out the back door following Dog. I was the last one out.

With my speed, I quickly overtook Jimmy and Dog. I was halfway down the hill before I looked over my shoulder and saw no sight of them. As scared as I was, there was no way I was gonna leave Jimmy to Bull, so I clenched my fists and started back up the hill. But I hadn't taken three steps before a great yowling came from the house and out the front door came a half dozen curling arms like tentacles or spider legs. They pulled the black mass of shadow out in their wake. Through the shadow, a pair of eyes fixed on me. I turned and ran down the hill towards the dancing men. I could hear the shadow behind me like fire's breath, its warmth too near.

I fled, though I had no destination. I ran through and around the dancing men. Maybe I was going in circles. I couldn't tell one dancing man from the next, and there were so many of them it was dizzying. But I knew I had to keep running. I heard the shadow man, I heard Bull, closing in like he was on all sides of me.

And where was Jimmy? *Shit, I've let him down. Fuck me, I've let him down again.*

The dancing men folded and fretted around me, their sounds like a chorus, a death chant for the living dead. By that point, I knew I was caught. Through the dancing men, I saw glimpses of shadow everywhere. I saw the shadow man to one side of me flare in his blackness and then vanish, and I saw Bull on the other, taking a step towards me with a dangerous nightmare face before he too vanished.

A wind of screams suddenly blew through the dancing men, screams of those the shadow man had imbibed. Before me, towering as tall as those balloons, was the shadow man, was Bull. I fell backwards, terrified. The shadow man reached for me, his tentacle arms ready to tear me apart, but then stopped only a few inches away.

"No," he spoke, his voice a rasping echo with elements of Bull and Patricia therein. "Wait. Deal with you later. First, the man. We need a host…"

"N-no!" I shouted. "Take me. Leave him alone."

But the shadow had lost interest in me for the moment. He grabbed one of the dancing men, arms and tentacles latching to it like a tar caterpillar, and forced himself inside. The dancing man struggled and then went solid and suddenly dark gray. And I swear, that balloon man now had a face, and it was full of menace and hate. One leg ripped itself from the fan, then the other, until the dark dancing man stood before me like a child's nightmare. Pushing the other dancing men out of its way, it made for the house. I followed, throwing rocks, sticks, anything I could find to get its attention, but nothing did the trick.

Then I heard the barking. Dog leapt seemingly out of nowhere, tackling the dancing man to the ground. That was the Dog I knew, his growls bringing back memories of… of…of what?

Dog snapped and bit and ripped at the dancing man. He tore half an arm right off. The dancing man howled, not in pain, but in anger, and threw Dog across the installation, where the hound crashed into another balloon and landed with a thud to the ground. He didn't move after that.

The dancing man was up again. My screaming and yelling did no good at all. He was intent on finding Jimmy. But it was Jimmy who found him.

"Hey! Stay Puft!" he yelled.

Jimmy was walking towards the dancing man, his shotgun in hand, like he could vanquish the dragon. But this dragon wasn't real, he had no substance. Jimmy could shoot holes in the dancing man all he wanted, but it would do nothing to the actual monster inside.

He stood facing the demon, and damn, didn't he look heroic. But he should have been running the other way. If I could have gotten to Jimmy in time, I might have even tried a possession and then run the hell out of that field of dancing men.

But before I could do anything, Jimmy glared at Bull, lifted the shotgun, and said, "Charlie boy, you've been a good son, and I love ya."

The bullet went straight through his head, and his body fell like a sack of potatoes to the ground. He had known Bull's intentions, and he wasn't gonna let it happen.

Bull yelled in anger. I howled in grief. Bull's attention was now again on me. He shredded the dancing man costume and was once more a towering black mass. But I was no longer fearful. I accepted my fate. I was, for lack of a better word, numb. I dropped to my knees, my eyes a blur, as I looked at Jimmy's motionless form on the ground. I felt the shadow fall over me, encompassing me in a painful embrace, bleeding me of my essence, of my soul, and beneath it all, I heard the combined cackling of a shadow man and Bull. They had won. I was breathing in the flames and the hate. I was floating in pieces of me.

Somewhere beyond me, in my periphery, there was a rising: a gray mass interspersed here and there with bright colors. At first, I thought it was the last flashes of a fevered consciousness, like when the synapses fires at death. But then I saw more clearly. Other dancing men were coming to life, ripping themselves from their fan bases and marching towards us. Some were gray, but others were colored most magnificently...like a carnival. Like carny spirits.

I hit the ground at once. Bull's hold on me lessened as the grays and the carnies set upon the black shadow. I crawled through the storm of rage as once again the grays began to tear asunder the shadow man. Without the help of the carnies, I doubt they would have lasted long. But the carnies tore into him even more ferociously, feeding on every sliver, not letting a single scrap get away this time. Bull was a screaming thunder in the valley as he was devoured. I saw no more of the shadow or the bully, as my vision was impeded by the circle of gray and colored dancing men as they fed.

My ears blocked the sound of Bull's mutilation, and my sight settled on Jimmy. He was still alive. Death, in whatever form it would choose to take, had not come for him, so I crawled, wounded, towards his body. I lay there, cradling his bloodied head, and I wept. He was my father, the only one I had ever known. The only one worth knowing, as far as I was concerned. And he was dying here in some meaningless field with a bunch of balloons and no Leroy to mourn him.

"Let me in," I whispered to him. "Let me in your head, Jimmy."

I was standing with Jimmy at the door inside his head now. We smiled at each other, a sad smile. Jimmy then looked at Leroy's door.

"Do ya think he would be happy with just the memory of me, Charlie boy?" His mind was quiet. There were no other voices. Everything was dimming; a darkness was creeping up the hallway.

"A memory is better than nothing at all, Jimmy," I replied. "I think in memories, things are sweeter, anyway. Smiles can be brighter."

"If I'm set to die tonight, I sure would like to see Leroy one more time."

"Then kick the door down, Jimmy."

"Will ya help me?"

"You bet."

"I love ya, Charlie boy. Ya know that, right?"

"Yeah. I know," I said, trying not to cry too much. "But dammit, you're a pain in the ass sometimes."

Jimmy laughed. "So Leroy is always tellin' me."

With that, we charged at the door and it buckled and busted with a great echoing crack. On the other side stood Leroy. He was in tears, and he grabbed us both in the biggest bearest of hugs. Then he kissed Jimmy. Over and over, he kissed him. They kissed each other. Strangely enough, there inside Leroy's head, my heart had never felt so full of love.

And then I found myself in the field again by Jimmy's body. My eyes were foggy. I saw the last of the grays, now done with the feast, move off into the night. The bodies of the dancing men lay littered around me and over the fans. My head began to grow light. But that couldn't be, because I had no head. I was a spirit.

I was a ghost.

I was a young man. And I died. Somehow. Somehow I died. How was it? How did that story go?

I forget.

* * * *

Charlie Boyd, for that was his given name, sat in the field beside his dying friend, at last forgetting the life he had known. Piece by piece, face by face, all the minutia of what had made him who he was had started falling away like a mask made of puzzle pieces. His memories began to resemble someone's fiction. Yet he knew enough to stay put. He knew this man, the name still echoing in his thoughts as "Jimmy," was of some importance. He knew this because his heart, or some semblance of feeling one could call a heart, still ached.

And then he saw a golden light rip through the very air right in front of him, like fabric being torn in a jagged line. The rip formed a tear, and the tear formed a hole, and into this hole, Charlie Boyd peered with immeasurable curiosity and saw what looked to be rollercoaster tracks circling and circling. And keeping his view focused on what was in the center of the tracks, he saw a beautiful field of golden barley. Charlie Boyd stood, sniffed back his tears, and walked closer for a better view.

"That's for you," came a voice from a young man who was suddenly standing right beside him. "You can go in now, Charlie. That's the Evermore, and it's all yours."

Charlie Boyd studied the young man. He recognized the face as one recognizes a character in a dream. The name came to him simply enough.

"Trent?" he said.

"No," said the Trent who was not Trent. "But he will be there. So will Alfie and everyone you have ever loved, everyone you've ever forgotten you've loved as well."

Charlie Boyd knew, his memories bubbling up every so often like last breaths, that he had not known a lot of love. He glanced back at Jimmy on the ground.

"I can't go," he said. "Not right now. I have this feeling… I need to see something through."

He hesitantly walked back to Jimmy, like he was a little lost boy, and when he looked again, the golden field of barley and the Trent who was not Trent were gone, the fabric of reality sealed up once again. Charlie Boyd was uncertain how long he would need to wait or, indeed, what he was waiting for, but Jimmy was important to him somehow. He saw flashes of that even as more and more bits of the mask fell away.

At last there was movement in the field, and a dog came hobbling towards them. He licked Jimmy's face and whined and then rested near them. Sometime later, a woman with a horrified expression came running through the field to find them as well. The dog licked her as she saw to Jimmy. There was some relief when Nessa determined he was alive. But that relief was quickly dampened by what that meant for him, what kind of life poor Jimmy would have from then on.

"Ya done your best," she said to Charlie Boyd in a defeatist tone of voice. "And it looks like ya might even have won. But damned if there wasn't a cost for that victory. Ya can go now, Charlie boy. Ain't no more for ya to do here."

But Charlie Boyd stayed just the same.

Nessa brought the Buick down into the valley, peeling through the field, destroying what was left of the art installation to get Jimmy to medical care. She stayed with Jimmy every day that first week in the hospital. He looked more machine than man. Nessa remained by his bedside like an old friend or a member of his family.

Charlie Boyd was no more than a presence in the room. At times, he was confused as to why he was there at all; it was like watching a television program to which he had no true connection. But eventually, a memory would come to him and keep him anchored for just a little bit longer.

Nessa would occasionally talk to Jimmy and even Charlie Boyd. Usually, this happened whenever she saw something of interest on the mounted television in the room. Charlie Boyd stood beside her as she watched the programs. He was dazzled by the displays of colors and sound coming from the large metal boxes. Nessa watched the news programs the most. Sometimes, though, she swept through the entertainment gossip shows, it seemed, just to feel a bit of superiority.

"Who is this fool?" she wondered aloud as a film director was being interviewed on one such program. "If he don't look possessed, then no one does. Don't ya agree, Charlie boy?"

The film director was talking, quite exuberantly, with eyes wide like he could see the future on a road right in front of him. He was going on and on about how he intended to reshoot a television serial he had made to some fanfare over thirty years ago, and how he was going to give it a brand-new ending, an ending deserving of the characters he had created. The interviewer seemed completely taken aback, salivating at having just broken this news.

Within a week, Leroy's sister Gladys arrived to visit Jimmy in the hospital. The doctor told her there was no hope for his recovery. She was startled at the sight of Nessa in the room with Jimmy, but said nothing of it. In time, the two began talking. Histories were revealed. Stories were told. A few days later, Nessa was there as Jimmy's comatose body was taken to its new home, a room in Leroy's family's mansion where he and Leroy could at last be together, side by side in their beds.

* * * *

So it happened that Charlie Boyd went walking one day and found himself, quite unintentionally, in a beautiful garden the likes of which he had never seen before. Pleasant songs drifted in the air along with butterflies and the scent of flowers and trees and, as he walked on, the delicious smell of good home cooking. The sound of rushing water drew him to a small falls near a large white gazebo wherein stood both Jimmy and Leroy, laughing and holding hands over a buffet of soul food. Charlie Boyd watched the two for a while before they took notice of him and immediately came forward to embrace him. Charlie Boyd was confused, but this affection made him smile. He knew these two men somehow. They were his last remaining memory, and it was a beautiful memory.

"Are ya leaving us, Charlie boy?" asked Jimmy. "Are ya goin' on at last?"

Both men had tears in their eyes, and so, Charlie Boyd noticed, did he.

"I think," he said. "I think I have to…"

"You're welcome to have lunch with us," said Leroy. "We got plenty."

"Naw. But thank you. I think I got someone waiting for me."

"Then you head on out, Charlie boy," said Leroy in his dark-timbered voice. "We'll see each other again someday. Yes, we will."

"What are…what will you two be doing until then?"

Jimmy and Leroy glanced at each other. "We have a whole lotta adventurin' to do," said Jimmy. "You go on now. You deserve the rest, Charlie."

Leroy gave Charlie Boyd a hug that would have broken a mortal man's back. "I'm gonna miss cookin' for ya. You was a real healthy eater. You was a real good boy."

"I was?" sputtered Charlie Boyd, his brow peaked with pain.

"Of course you was," said Jimmy. "You was the best."

"Now you git," said Leroy, his voice cracking. "Ya can't get to Heaven while piddlin' around in someone else's head. Wave goodbye to Charlie, Jimmy."

And that was the last Charlie Boyd saw of his family. In that life.

* * * *

He walked to where the old house stood now overlooking the valley where the dancing men had been. The place was falling apart. In a few years, it would be demolished and questions of its origin would become something of local folklore.

And there, on the same spot in the field where Charlie Boyd had gotten his second glimpse of the Evermore, he saw it for the third time as it tore through the air. The field of barley glowed, and this time someone called to him from the other side. Charlie Boyd could see Trent standing there in the tall golden grain, waiting for him. Charlie Boyd smiled, and with a laugh as innocent as a child's, he stepped out of this world and into the next.

The End

Trademark Acknowledgement

Eric Arvin

Eric Arvin resides in the same sleepy Indiana river town where he grew up. He graduated from Hanover College with a Bachelors in History. He has lived, for brief periods, in Italy and Australia. He has survived brain surgery and his own loud-mouthed personal demons. Eric is the author of *Woke Up In A Strange Place, Subsurdity, Simple Men, Galley Proof,*and various other sundry and not-so-sundry writings. He intends to live the rest of his days with tongue in cheek and eyes set to roam.

Also by Eric Arvin

Azrael and the Light Bringer
The Mingled Destinies of Crocodiles and Men
SubSurdity: Vignettes from Jasper Lane
Suburbilicious: Vignettes from Jasper Lane
Simple Men
Another Enchanted April
Woke Up in a Strange Place
Galley Proof
SuburbaNights
Kid Christmas Rides Again
Man Falls Down

She's Come Undone
Miss Locks
Roids, Rumps & Revenge

Anthologies:
Zombie Boyz
Slight Details & Random Events
Mr. Right Now
Uniform Appeal
Erotica Exotica: Tales of Sex, Magic, & the Supernatural

Comic Books:
The Blackbeard Legacy

Lightning Source UK Ltd.
Milton Keynes UK
UKOW05f0136211114

241949UK00001BA/22/P